AMETHYST MOON

AMETHYST MOON
A CLIFTON NOVELLA

DARA GIRARD

ISBN: 978-1949764840

AMETHYST MOON

ILORI PRESS BOOKS, LLC

www.iloripressbooks.com

BOOKS BY DARA GIRARD

Duvall Sisters

The Glass Slipper Project

Taming Mariella

A Reluctant Hero

The Black Stockings Society

Power Play

A Gentleman's Offer

Body Chemistry

Round the Clock

Return of the Black Stockings Society

Playing for Keeps

After Hours

A Private Affair

Just One Look

Private Lessons

Ladies of the Pen

Words of Seduction

Pages of Passion

Beneath the Covers

Henson Series

Table for Two

Gaining Interest

Careless Rapture

Dangerous Curves

Familiar Stranger

It Happened One Wedding

Unexpected Pleasure

Midnight Promise

Sweet Temptation

Always and Forever

Clifton Sisters

The Sapphire Pendant

The Amber Stone

The Emerald Ring

Fortune Brothers

A Tempting Proposal

A Seductive Arrangement

Novels

Honest Betrayal

The Daughters of Winston Barnett

Remember My Name

Illusive Flame

Winterwood Lane

CHAPTER ONE

He had no name.

He just appeared one night in one of those cool, fairy tale-like dreams that don't make sense at first. One where she was at one moment floating in a blue sky with marshmallow white clouds then moments, later prostrate on a pine strew ground in the middle of a dark forest as if called by an invisible force.

She felt no sensation of falling. No fear, no uneasiness, just curiosity. She didn't know how she got there or why she was lying on the ground. She lifted her head and pulled a wet brown leaf off of her cheek and glanced around.

A soft darkness surrounded her. The faint sunlight found pockets between the canopy of trees, creating odd patterns of amorphous grey shapes on a well-trodden path. The path cut through the forest like a dried-up riverbed-- long and narrow.

She slowly rose to her feet.

The forest held the strange, sacred silence of a cemetery.

A slight breeze toyed with the hem of her white dress and brushed the back of her neck.

She realized her pressed black hair, which usually fell past her shoulders, was pulled up in a French twist held up by a large clip. She took a step forward and noticed her shoes. She wore slippers but didn't seem to feel the ground; none of the mud touched the satin surface. Wait? Satin shoes in the forest? That definitely didn't make sense.

Nothing felt familiar and yet she didn't feel afraid.

Until he appeared.

Olivia hadn't heard him. The ghostly silence growing more evident as she became more attuned to what she hadn't heard—no birdsong, no rustling of leaves, no scurrying animals. Complete eerie silence. So why hadn't she sensed anything? Why hadn't she heard even the faintest footstep before he stepped out from behind a large oak tree with the swift mastery of a wizard?

He appeared as a giant shadow at first, the darkness embracing him more than the slivers of light.

He stood large, still, silent.

She hesitated not sure what to do. What was he doing there? Why was he blocking her path?

"You shouldn't be here," the man finally said, his deep voice carrying a dark warning.

"I'm not lost," she heard her dreamself say and only after she said the words did they feel true. She wasn't lost. She didn't feel uncertain or uneasy about the forest. She had a sense she was supposed to be there, even though she didn't know where 'here' was exactly. She didn't feel uneasy about anything.

Only about him.

He wasn't supposed to be there.

"I'm alright," she said, taking a step forward with a false bravado, hoping he would let her pass.

He didn't move.

Olivia swallowed and took another step forward. There was enough space on the path to go around him.

She didn't want to turn back. Something inside her, or the dream person in her, told her that she had to keep walking, get past him. That what she needed was on the other side.

She continued to walk towards him, the shadows fading and giving her a better sense of the man. The darkness making way for the shape of broad shoulders in a loose fitting cotton shirt of another age, powerful legs clad in jeans, a towering height and skin as brown as the trunks of the trees that surrounded them.

Her heart pounded, with one more step she would be beside him and then—

He moved in front of her—quick, smooth, determined—causing her to cry out in surprise and stumble back.

Brown eyes that seemed to gleam with an unknown power, met hers, pinning her in place.

"If you're going to be foolish at least take a weapon," he said.

"A weapon?"

"For the journey."

Journey? How did he know she was on a journey? "Who are you?"

"Turn back."

"I asked you a question."

"Doesn't matter, my advice is still the same."

She didn't feel foolish, but she did begin to question why she would need a weapon.

"What would you suggest?"

For some reason the question surprised him. He hesitated before he said, "Come back and I'll fashion something for you."

Fashion, not make. What an odd turn of phrase. And why would he assume she'd be able to come back?

She couldn't come back. It was a dream. She'd never have this dream again.

"I won't be coming back."

"I hope not," he said after a long sigh. "It's dangerous."

"But it's just a dream."

He briefly glanced away, muttered something she couldn't hear before he looked at her again. "Dreams can become nightmares."

The words were meant to frighten her, but they had the opposite effect. They made her see him more clearly, as if more of the shadows continued to fall away and she noticed the shape of his lips. There wasn't much to them, and he had more of a fierce face than a handsome one, but although his eyes were dark and intense, they held a kindness.

She had no reason to fear him. Instead he feared for her.

She reached out to touch him and he quickly stepped back. A realization swept through her—he always feared her. She sensed that she was a danger to him and he knew it. But why?

What was there to fear?

"It's late," he said, "If you return, I'll have something for you."

She didn't want to wake up. She didn't want to not see him again.

"It's not late let's—"

"Please."

His plea sounded like an order and she found the intensity of the forest waver as if a pebble had disturbed the clear surface image reflected in a lake.

She felt the pull of a new awareness.

She was waking up.

Soon she would leave the dreamscape. And him.

But she didn't want to. She wanted to make this moment last.

"Who are you?" she said in a breathless rush.

The shadows around him grew, moments later he was a giant shadow again, with a deep voice that said, "Careful on your way home."

Ordinary words that held a strange power: one of protection, of care, of careful command.

"Will I see you again?" she asked as the forest continued to dissolve into meaningless shapes.

She saw his mouth move, saw the briefest glint of white teeth curved into a smile before she woke up.

His answer lost to the dreamscape and memory.

SHE WOKE up with an aching longing. What was that?

It embarrassed her how much her dream had affected her. How she already missed him. As if he were real. How she wished she could close her eyes and summon him at will. But of course she couldn't. She was terrible at drawing so she couldn't even sketch his face as reference. When she was fully awake her simple, ordinary existence made it clear how much of a fantasy he was.

No one had ever made her feel like this.

Little did she know that the fantasy would return night after night. Sometimes she met him at the tip of a lake with obsidian waters reflecting an evening sky with no moon or stars, only dotted with the bright glow of fireflies, and his warning was still the same. But most nights, she found herself in the same forest. And on one of those nights the forest sun would touch the edge of a pendant he wore around his neck. She saw a crescent moon with an amethyst stone perched in the curve of it. It felt familiar.

She pointed. "What is that?"

The man lifted the pendant in the palm of his hand and gazed at it, pensive. "A gift," he said before he did something truly remarkable.

He met her gaze and slowly smiled, stealing her heart and claiming it as his own.

OLIVIA WOKE up and came to two realizations that morning. The first was that her dreams had become a sanctuary she sought every night. But the second realization was something she'd never anticipated.

She realized that no matter how cute an animal was, or how much that animal made her laugh, how soft its fur was, or how the silly grin on its face made Olivia smile.

Never, ever agree to look after a dog nicknamed Houdini.

CHAPTER TWO

She didn't come to that realization at first. It took a while.

Olivia woke that morning feeling sore and tired and not sure why. The house was blanketed in a strange quiet. Usually Daisy, the shaggy brown mutt she was looking after over the summer, would notice she was awake and come bounding through the door like a kid spying Santa Claus. The lively dog would jump on the bed and greet her with a warm wet lick on the cheek and sometimes an odorless fart for good measure.

But there was no bounding, dashing, nothing but silence.

Olivia brushed her teeth then padded downstairs calling out the dog's name.

Was she hiding?

In the kitchen, she picked up the wedding invitation she'd tossed there the previous afternoon. The sight of it made her inwardly tremble with fear.

Where others may see a beautifully rendered, painted floral design on pulpy handmade paper, she saw teeth.

Tiny little teeth that she imagined penetrating into her skin, slowly chomping their way through her veins until they reached her heart, where they could find a soft, vulnerable section of her heart and let their pointed edges take a bite, leaving her bleeding internally.

Olivia set the invitation on the counter next to the other three she'd received. She regretted forwarding her mail to the house where she was dog sitting.

The house sat near the center of a quaint Maryland town most people enjoyed escaping from during the summer months for more exotic locations. Most tourists passed through on their way to more exciting destinations like Ocean City or Catlon Bay without noticing the town's colorful main street dotted with historic brick buildings or carefully manicured lawns.

Olivia enjoyed the anonymity the town provided her. At home, she felt the baggage of her past failures shining behind every smile or glance of the people she knew.

This house and town offered her a brief respite from life. It would have been so much easier to ignore the invitations if she hadn't known they'd existed.

But she'd thought it would have been irresponsible to be away for nearly four months and not keep track of her friends.

Although, right now having friends felt like a liability.

She felt as if she were drowning in invitations to weddings, baby showers, housewarmings, pet adoptions, graduations, job promotions.

Everyone had exciting, life-changing news.

Everyone except her.

Especially not the news she'd hoped to have shared by now.

News of her wedding day.

Her family prided themselves of being one of the stars in the Caribbean community, but Olivia's lack of status or raising achievement was proving to be an embarrassment.

She pushed the stack aside and filled Daisy's food and water bowls. She shook the dry food in the metal bowl, expecting Daisy to come running.

But she didn't.

The silence grew with the edge of panic as a terrible thought gripped her. No. It couldn't be. Impossible. Daisy had escaped? How could it be? She'd made sure to lock up everywhere. She was responsible. That was why people trusted her. How could this have happened?

She checked every door, all locked. The windows were fastened shut. The dog had to be somewhere.

But she wasn't.

Olivia raced through the two-level cottage style house. Up and down the stairs.

She imagined having to post flyers along the charming residential street lined with evergreen magnolias. Make a plea online. What if...

No. She wouldn't panic. The dog had to be okay.

First she'd walk the neighborhood then she'd post a notice on the neighborhood forum, possibly put up flyers if necessary. But she didn't want to do that yet. Not if she didn't have—

The alarm on her phone alerted her to an appointment.

She swore at the sight of the reminder. How could she

have missed this? She'd forgotten she had a blind date today. She only had two hours to prepare before the lunch date (dinner would have been too formal and breakfast was definitely out of the question). Her mother had set it up and she couldn't cancel. Because Olivia had bowed out of two other set-ups, her mother had threatened to create a profile for Olivia on ten different dating sites if she did.

Plus, this could be her chance. The chance of finding love. To break what had felt like a curse. Then she'd have news of her own. Perhaps she'd end up with a date to take to some of these weddings and events. She wouldn't have to arrive beautifully dressed (to avoid looks of pity), hair and makeup perfectly rendered but subtle (to avoid jealousy) alone.

Olivia raced to her bedroom and flew open the closet doors and started to dress. She searched for her favorite scarf then frowned when she couldn't find it. The dog wasn't the only thing that had gone missing. In the past couple of days she'd misplaced a necklace, socks, earrings and now this scarf. She couldn't imagine why.

But she'd find them.

It would all work out.

She briefly glanced out the window. The white and blue house rested like a contented cat, its white wraparound porch resembling a grin, on the corner of the street. From her vantage point on the upper floor she could see down into her neighbor's backyard. A circular wrought iron table and two matching chairs gave an illusion of order to what appeared to be a wild field of weeds—a mixture of dandelions and ground ivy. A few valiant, overgrown azalea bushes tried to offer a semblance of a garden along with a crooked pinwheel near the back door. Olivia could imagine Daisy finding adventure there, but she didn't see the dog or anyone else.

She turned from the window with a sigh.

The dog would show up, she'd done so before. Her owner had laughed about it. *Daisy always finds her way home.* Then she'd find that she'd put those missing items in some strange location she hadn't thought about and she'd have a fabulous date.

Olivia put on her lipstick and smiled. She couldn't risk missing a chance at happiness.

CHAPTER THREE

But nearly three hours later, as Olivia sat in a fine dining restaurant amid elegantly-dressed patrons and their tittering laughter, surrounded by exquisite art-inspired cuisine and accompanied by a handsome man in a designer suit, she faced a painful reckoning.

They'd lied to her. All of them. Her parents, her teachers, her friends.

Movies, books, articles.

Adverts, songs.

Everything. Everyone. Everywhere.

It had all been a lie and she'd believed it.

She'd believed that being beautiful and good and kind would be rewarded. That she'd meet someone and have a wonderful life with them.

But it had been the biggest lie of all.

Olivia sipped her dry white wine and nodded at the man in front of her, wondering how a minute could feel like centuries. She didn't say anything, she didn't have to. Her date hadn't stopped talking about himself for the past half hour. She'd laughed at jokes that weren't funny and pretended to be interested in a man who had to recall, in excruciating detail, his time as a student at Stanford and NYU.

Only once did she entertain the thought of excusing herself and leaving, but she'd been raised to always consider the other person's feelings, even if the effort wasn't reciprocated or even considered.

She'd hoped he'd be the one. Or at least a potential.

Because she wanted what so many others had—a family. A husband, a couple kids, a nice house.

But while she remained good and sweet, not to mention beautiful, everyone liked to mention that as if that was the most important part of her (and if her mother was to have any say it would be), she'd watched her plain faced cousins each find men who loved them: From the hotheaded Jessie, to chubby, odd Teresa, and cool, calm Michelle. Each had found men who looked past their flaws (strikingly more than a few. Aside from their lack of looks they each had strange gifts—one could read stones, another had an ability to heal or something and Olivia could never really figure out what Michelle's gift was and never wanted to ask) while she was normal.

Beautiful and normal.

It felt like a curse.

She plastered on a well-practiced smile as her date began to tell her about his recent trip to Iceland.

She held back a yawn, the effort making her eyes water.

Perhaps she could tolerate boring. Her date owned a three bedroom house in a desirable zip code and he could take her away from the tiny apartment she'd managed to find and the neighbor who occasionally made lewd comments when she saw him.

Jokes she always smiled and laughed off because he always reminded her he was 'just kidding'.

She wasn't an interesting person so perhaps it was good that her date didn't ask her any questions about herself. What could she say?

Olivia gazed down at the dainty squares she'd fashioned so that she could eat her roasted trout and quinoa without ruining her lipstick or making her cheeks bulge. Her mother had drilled into her the proper way to eat. Take small bites, chew gently (not like a cow chewing cud) and swallow. Eat sparingly so that you can leave room for dessert that you won't eat.

She never really understood the last part (why should she have to skip dessert?) but her mother said it showed constraint and that many men liked that. She was encouraged to offer to take it home (ordering dessert and then let it sit there would have been wanton wasting behavior she couldn't do) or have him eat it (showing generosity and a willingness to put his needs above her own).

Her mother told her that most men wouldn't notice she didn't eat the dessert and, to her horror, her mother was right.

But Olivia was still hungry and the thought of even pretending to order dessert so that she could spend more time with this man depressed her.

Why hadn't she met anyone yet? It wasn't that she hadn't had interest from anyone. When you're attractive you get noticed but not always the way you want.

She'd gotten interest from older men willing to make her a happy trophy wife, younger men who wouldn't mind her as a mistress, single men who weren't ready for marriage but liked to have something nice on their arm for different events, lonely men who only wanted companionship, horny men who wanted sex for the price of a meal at Arby's.

She was sick of being pitied. Her mother wondered what was wrong.

"You were given this face for a reason," her mother lamented one spring morning when she'd stopped by to visit, catching Olivia before she could slip out the back of her apartment building and avoid her. "You're not using your looks to its full potential."

Why did the problem have to be her?

She glanced over at a couple laughing.

She turned and looked out the window in disgust and envy.

"Would you like dessert?"

Olivia turned sharply to him, surprised. It was the first question he'd asked her all afternoon.

She should get back to see if Daisy had returned home.

She should stop pretending there was even a chance for this date to become a relationship.

She should say no.

But she wanted to give him a chance to prove her wrong. To have something to tell her mother and prove that the world was wrong. She'd done everything she could: Singles events, dating sites, blind dates. Nothing had come from them and she was no longer desperate.

But, she hadn't given up—yet.

"Sure," she said and regretted it even more when he smiled and picked up the menu.

She'd made a mistake.

Because it had all been a lie.

And there was no one to talk to. No one would sympathize with an attractive woman, with a decent job, having a terrible love life. They'd think she was bragging.

But she wasn't bragging. She wanted to find someone who could understand.

Unfortunately, nobody did. So she was alone and she would remain alone.

She'd accept that.

She'd give up.

Today was the last time she'd endure a date like this.

She'd give up on dreams of love and marriage and finding the right man.

Waking dreams proved painful. But at night, she waited for him. The love of her life that had no name, but always made her feel safe, that cared about her. He felt more real than anyone.

That was where she belonged.

CHAPTER FOUR

Garrett Williams could pinpoint the exact moment—-to a precise second on a wintry day—-when everything changed. The moment when he realized something was very, very wrong with him and his life would never be the same.

It descended swiftly, quietly and settled without him knowing about it until it was too late.

It was a moment when he stopped feeling anything.

To say he felt numb would have been charitable. It was worse than that. He could still feel the cold brisk morning of a Maryland winter, or the syrup ladened humidity of a summer, but inside the hospital doors where he worked as an ER nurse was where the feelings stopped.

Nothing touched him. Someone died. Someone lived. He felt the same about both.

As if nothing mattered. That's when he knew he was in trouble because, for him, nothing he did, nothing he said, nothing he offered, nothing mattered.

The never-ending demands for care and compassion had worn him down until both had run dry, leaving him as parched as the Kalahari Desert.

He'd never thought it would happen to him. He was usually the most caring guy in any group. Even as a kid his friends would tell him their pains and he'd listen and comfort them. The day his sister damaged her ACL and realized her dream of becoming a professional basketball player was over, he'd let her cry on his shoulder and she'd always told him that she wouldn't have known how to go on without him.

The day his friend had lost his beloved seizure alert dog to a brain tumor, Garrett was one of the few people his friend trusted to share his pain. "You understand," his friend kept repeating, "You never make me feel ashamed to feel sad, to feel lost. It's a gift."

A gift Garrett had lost.

Sure, he still managed to smile. Sure, he did his rounds. His new feelings hadn't affected his work. To his horror he felt he was more efficient. Perhaps that's why they'd given him two new patients when a fellow nurse had not shown up. There was no mistake that they were understaffed. They'd already had three excellent nurses retire.

He remembered Stella, a fellow nurse, saying they should come up with a campaign begging the retiring nurses to stay, and Garrett had laughed because he knew he was supposed to, but again he felt nothing. They were leaving. He liked them. It was over. Move on.

Move on.

That's all he did nowadays. That's how he got through every day. Soon the days had started to blend into each other.

Each patient became an ailment, a disease, not a face, certainly not a name.

Names felt like too much of a burden and he began to use them as quick identifiers, like a store clerk putting SKUs on different cans of fruit.

It wasn't one moment that told him he should take a break, but a series of little warnings he ignored until the morning he woke up and fell flat on his face.

His legs completely gave out. He lay on the floor. He didn't even have the ability to laugh at such an ignoble morning pratfall. That still didn't shock him, it was that he lay there on the hardwood floor and realized he didn't have the strength to get up.

He was too tired.

Too drained.

He didn't want to go to work.

The work he used to love.

So he decided to take his vacation time and try to recover even a part of himself. Although he'd gotten to the point he wasn't sure he could recover. He feared he'd worked past his ability to be human. That this robotic feeling would stay.

His aunts and grandmother suggested he find a nice Trinny girl and finally settle down. As if finding some Trinidadian beauty would make the empty feeling disappear. He'd been in two previous long-term relationships that he knew from the outset wouldn't go anywhere, but he didn't want to be alone. He never had the energy to end them, putting the burden on someone else to admit the relationship was over. He took refuge in blaming his work schedule for the demise of each relationship, not wanting to admit that his heart really hadn't been in them.

That bothered him too. He could understand his personal life not working out, but his professional life had been his identity. It made him feel better and more useful than he really was. Without it...he saw all his flaws and short-coming and thought of the people he may have hurt without meaning to. Caring at a distance felt easier than caring up close. But now he couldn't even do that.

But on the second week of his self-imposed vacation, where he'd spent most of his time heating up frozen meals and lazing on the couch watching movies he quickly forgot about once they ended, thinking about a walk on a beach somewhere (a holiday he was too tired to plan for, let alone book), he'd suffered a night that completely stole sleep away from him.

An unsettling incident that would be the first of many that he'd grown accustomed to as much as he also dreaded and anticipated them.

He tried to sleep in the day, but rest still continued to elude him, so he decided to take a walk in the neighborhood.

That's when the sight of a scruffy little mutt changed the direction of his life.

CHAPTER FIVE

Houdini was home.

Olivia nearly dropped her dessert when she saw her.

She rushed forward surprised to see the dog tied to the post on the porch steps. In front of the dog sat two bowls filled with fresh water and food. Someone had taken care to find the dog and look after it.

Her joy slowly dropped to dread as a thought struck her.

She quickly pulled out her phone. Had someone tried to reach her? Or rather Daisy's owner? Had they left messages?

Olivia checked her phone expecting to see a series of missed calls from her friend. She could imagine voice mails insisting that Olivia tell her what was going on, asking her how she'd managed to let Daisy get loose (while also recanting for the hundredth time how she'd managed to do the same) and that some stranger had contacted her.

But, to Olivia's relief, she didn't see anything. With a quick prayer of thanks and a heavy sigh, she put her phone away. At least the Good Samaritan hadn't let anyone else know. But that also meant she didn't know who to thank. Too bad.

She was just grateful that the dog was safely home.

"Where did you go off to?" Olivia asked, undoing the knot the stranger had used. It was a quick-release knot that easily came loose and yet had held the dog snugly, but not too tight, until she'd returned to undo it. She'd never seen a knot like that before.

Daisy gave her a smug happy grin then licked her face.

"I'm going to be more careful this time. Come on."

Olivia went inside and took off her shoes, releasing another sigh of relief. The date was over, Daisy was home. All was well.

Then the phone rang.

She saw the number on her mobile and groaned.

She'd gotten to the point where she dreaded the phone ringing. The sound of her mother's voice on the other end always came with the typical refrain:

Have you met anyone yet?

What are you doing? Your sisters and brother are happily married now. I thought you would have been one of the first. You weren't born this beautiful for no reason.

Her mother never asked Olivia how she was. How her day or week had been. Olivia could have saved a child from drowning, rescued someone from a burning building, created a system that lifted millions out of poverty, or ended world hunger and none of those feats would have been enough.

She could imagine her mother saying in clipped, polite tones, "That's very nice dear, but have you met someone yet?"

It wasn't enough that her mother had persuaded her to move to Catlon Bay so that her cousin's husband, Kenneth, could introduce her to all the right people. He'd tried, of course, until the scandal about his background and parentage soon followed and scared away some of her chances. Not that she minded. Olivia liked Kenneth and anyone who didn't want to associate with her because of his parentage was not someone she wanted to know.

Not that she'd ever tell her mother that. Her mother cared about bloodlines, class, status.

Olivia had meant to care too and did up to a point. Her cousin, Jessie, had found happiness with Kenneth and cousin Teresa had married a man with a shady background and odd mannerisms that Olivia still found strangely disarming and didn't know why.

Michelle had married well from the get go and reunited with her estranged husband.

They were all well matched.

But Olivia felt as if she had a neon sign that pointed to an obvious flaw everyone else could see but her.

She was beautiful, but she wasn't vain about it. She was cordial, pleasant, engaging. Sure she liked pretty, expensive things, was that a crime?

Olivia's love of fashion had helped her snag two retail jobs until a newly married head manager didn't like how often her new husband "stopped by" to see how his wife was doing and ended up chatting with Olivia instead.

So Olivia was taken off the floor to handle the stock until she found herself covering up the mistakes of another employee so often that she ended up doing overtime, for which she wasn't compensated, and decided to quit. The second retail job was in an upscale store with a lazy supervisor (who always conveniently disappeared at crucial moments) and entitled customers (who tended to have a round of tantrums every other day). She decided to quit there too.

She didn't know what to do with herself. She had no real aspirations. She hadn't been raised to have them and hadn't thought she'd need to. She wasn't academic, although she was smart. She never thought she'd own a business like Michelle or freelance like Teresa.

She felt lost. Who was she supposed to be?

She'd taken the house/dog-sitting job to give herself some time to think. To be away from the constant reminder that everyone, or at least almost everyone, was happily paired. But the afternoon lunch disaster hadn't provided the respite she'd hoped for. Getting out of town hadn't quite worked either. Problems seemed to follow her.

The phone fell silent then rang again. Olivia sighed and answered, but before she could say a word, her mother said, "How did it go? Are you going to see him again?"

Olivia briefly closed her eyes, she thought of lying, but knew her mother would follow up and make sure she did. "I don't think so."

"Never mind."

Olivia nearly dropped her phone. It wasn't like her mother to be so calm. "Really?"

"Yes."

Could it be her mother had given up? That she would give her some space that she would—

"There is someone I would like you to meet."

Olivia sat down hard onto the stiff teal colored sofa (it

was an expensive designer piece as comfortable as two boards of plywood) and shook her head. She should have known better. "Another time."

"You don't have time."

"Mom, please." Olivia felt Daisy brush her shaggy head against her thigh. She bent and stroked the dog, grateful for the distraction. "Could we discuss this later? I only got in from the other date and—"

"It's always 'another time,'" her mother said in clipped tones, revealing hints of her upbringing in England with a touch of the Caribbean in the vowels. "I don't think you have the luxury to keep putting this off." Olivia inwardly sighed. She was a shade past thirty and her mother made her feel ancient. "What could possibly keep you so busy?"

"As I said, I only got in from another—"

"Do you want to get married?"

"Yes, you know I do."

"I just wondered, because finding the right match takes effort. Lots of effort. It's not for the faint of heart and it's been a while since—"

"Mom, I really need to—"

"I haven't finished."

"I'm sorry."

"How dare you cut me off when I haven't finished speaking."

Olivia bit her lip.

"Heartbreak is well and good for awhile, but it won't get you far."

"I know." She paused when she noticed something bright pink in the dog's fur. She pulled it off and noticed it was a small yellow flower petal. What adventures had the dog been up to?

"Pining for a man—"

Olivia looked at the back of the petal hoping Daisy hadn't done too much damage to someone's garden. "I'm not pining."

Her mother sharply inhaled her breath, outraged. "You've done it again."

Olivia squeezed her eyes shut. "I'm sorry."

"To think I raised a daughter with such poor manners. One who cuts me off when I'm in midsentence? What's gotten into you?"

She stared at the petal and thought about the man in her dreams. One she looked forward to seeing each night. It was not something she could tell anyone. "I'm sorry."

"You should be. Treating your mother, who loves you, like this."

Olivia knew there was nothing she could say to appease her so she stayed silent.

"Next Saturday no excuses," her mother said then gave Olivia the address of the restaurant, which was an hour's drive away.

"If you give me his information, I can contact him myself. You really don't need to be there."

"You don't want to see me?"

"I don't want you to put yourself out."

"I don't mind. I'll do anything for my children."

Except leave them alone. Her mother lived in Pennsylvania, hours away from Olivia's apartment in Maryland, but at times like this her mother made her feel as if she lived only across the county line instead of in another state.

Olivia and her siblings used to joke that their mother would weather a blizzard and a journey from Maine to Georgia to make sure her offspring was suitably paired.

"I only want to see you happy," her mother said.

"Of course," Olivia said, when in truth she wanted to say, "I'm not unhappy because I don't have someone, I'm unhappy that *you're* unhappy that I don't have someone." But she'd stopped being truthful with her mother years ago so she cheerily said, "Goodbye."

While her fear continued to grow.

She feared that unhappiness would follow her. There had been moments, several in fact, when she liked being by herself and that just wasn't normal for most. Her mother liked to imagine that Olivia filled the role of a broken hearted woman who'd suffered a grand tragic romance, but the truth was it had been much more pedantic.

Olivia had dated a man she'd hoped to marry for about eighteen months. He'd proposed, she'd dutifully accepted and then one day he'd gotten mad at her over dinner and grabbed her plate, spat in her food then mixed it in and told her to eat it.

She didn't.

He called her a prude since, as he put it, they'd swapped more than spit in the past. (He'd claimed he'd lost a bucket full of semen, but he tended to exaggerate).

She called him a pig. He spat in her face and stormed off.

The following day he arrived on her doorstep with a dozen red roses and a pearl necklace, which she firmly, but politely, refused.

She returned the engagement ring and never spoke to him again.

However, she gave her mother a very abridged version of the events so, in her mother's thoughts, he was the one who got away.

Truth was, Olivia envied her cousins' special abilities. Her line of the family was ordinary (which suited them perfectly, thank you very much) and she was only beautiful (like a garden, a vase, nothing more interesting). At times Olivia pictured herself on someone's shelf as a display. Would anyone want her for more than that? Did she have anything to offer?

Trapped. That's how her life had started to feel. From one disastrous date to another. She wondered if her life would ever feel like her own.

She disconnected and set her phone down then went to the kitchen ready to eat her dessert.

CHAPTER SIX

The forest stood silent, engulfed in a soft pink mist that smelled like strawberries.

Olivia moved along the path, her satin clad feet silent against the ground.

She walked, anticipating, hoping, wishing, to see the man again.

But as the mist shifted from a strawberry haze to a cool grey mist her hopes dimmed. She glanced at every tree hoping to see his shadow.

"You shouldn't be here."

The voice came from behind her. She spun around, but didn't see anything. She recognized his tone and warning, but this time it sounded more urgent.

"Where are you?" she asked.

"I'm here," he said, but his voice felt far away rather than close.

"Let me see you."

He didn't reveal himself. She noted a tense pause before he said, "It's dangerous."

"To see you?"

"For you to be here."

"You keep saying that and yet—"

"Here we are," he finished, sounding resigned.

"Exactly." She slowly spun around in the circle. "Where are you?"

"Like I said, I'm here."

"Then why can't I see you?"

Another pause before he said, "I'm behind you."

Olivia turned and saw him leaning against a tree with his arms folded. She took a step towards him, relieved to see him again, but he held up a hand. "That's close enough."

She took another cautious step closer. "But I can hardly see you properly in this mist."

"That's okay."

But it wasn't. She wanted to be closer, nearer. She wanted this. Wanted him.

Didn't he want her?

Would she be rejected even in this dream landscape? What was wrong with her?

It was only when he said, "Nothing," that she realized she'd spoken aloud. "It's just not safe."

"It feels safe and it's only a dream. Why wouldn't it be safe?"

He lowered his gaze.

"You don't find me attractive?"

His gaze met hers, his sharp brown eyes seeming to pierce through the mist and hold her captive. "I do."

"Desirable?"

He nodded.

She walked up to him, drawn to his quiet power. "And I feel the same. Kiss me."

He pressed his fingers against her lips. "You haven't considered something."

"What?"

"That the most dangerous part of this forest could be me."

She had considered that but still had no desire to turn away because she wanted to feel something, even if it was fear.

The emotions he brought forth from her made her feel alive.

He could be the most dangerous part, but she knew he wasn't.

And fear wasn't what she felt when she was with him.

Olivia captured his mouth before he could protest. This was her dream, her rules. He would be the prey, she the predator. No more waiting, no more patience. She would seize this man now.

She tasted his surprise, his hunger, his desire.

And woke up aroused, satiated, longing, weak.

The space beside her was empty and cold when briefly she'd expected it to feel warm. Her dreams were so vivid, so real she'd imagined she could conjure them into reality.

Especially the man. Such detail to a face she'd never seen before. He felt so real, so familiar. Why?

Olivia stretched her arms, softly groaning at how sore they felt, and then heard the silence, which made her heart sink.

The silence only meant one thing: Houdini was gone again.

CHAPTER SEVEN

What were the odds?

She wouldn't panic, the little mischievous mutt would return.

But Olivia couldn't understand how the dog managed to do it. All the doors were fastened closed, the windows too. How could the dog leave without setting off the alarm?

Last night, Olivia had briefly woken up because she'd thought she'd heard a noise. She'd groggily checked outside, but hadn't seen anything and hadn't noticed Daisy dashing past her. She'd been certain Daisy had been sound asleep in her dog bed where she'd left her.

She would have noticed if Daisy had gotten out that way.

Olivia changed into jeans and a cream colored shirt ready to search for her. She put on a pair of gold hoop earrings and absently noticed a bracelet missing but didn't want to think about it.

She walked the perimeter of the house to see if there was a loose panel, a secret tunnel, something—anything!—to explain the dog's extraordinary disappearing acts. But she couldn't find anything.

She walked the length of the neighborhood and returned empty handed.

She hoped that either the dog would return or another Good (possibly the same?) Samaritan would return her. For now she had to get some items from the local hardware store. One would be a bell to attach to the dog's collar so that Olivia could always know where Daisy was, then perhaps a trap to figure out where the dog was escaping from.

SHE REGRETTED ASKING the store clerk for help finding where they kept free standing pet gates. The eager to please young man, with a closely shaved head and silver hoop earring, was now following her around asking her if she needed anything else and offering suggestions.

"And we also have eco-friendly poop bags..."

Oh, please go away. "I really don't need anything else," Olivia said politely.

"And amazing beddings even though we're not a pet store."

Olivia nodded trying to think of the best way to gently get him to leave her alone, as well as hoping someone else would ask for his help, when she heard a voice.

That voice. *His voice.*

A voice that made her think of soft pink mists and dark paths in a forest.

Her heart raced. How was that possible?

"And we have a bunch of pet friendly plants," the clerk was saying.

"I really don't need anything else, thank you."

He still didn't look like he planned to leave. When he opened his mouth she feared he was going to ask for her number. "I really have to go," she said, "excuse me."

She dashed into the other aisle, closer to where she'd first heard the voice, but the low murmur of sounds didn't register. None of them were his. Had he left the store? Had it all been in her mind?

And then she heard it again. This time the voice was followed by a slight laugh—low, mischievous.

That sound was unfamiliar. He never laughed. Or at least she'd never heard it before. Olivia turned the corner and saw the back of a man's head.

He was just as she'd pictured him. Big, broad shouldered, brown skinned with short black hair. Now, if she could only see his face.

Olivia began to follow him then stopped after a few steps. What was wrong with her? What would she do when she caught up with him? What if he was there with someone?

She didn't know this man. It didn't matter that he sounded like someone in her dream. Dreams weren't real. No matter how much she wanted them to be. No matter how real they had started to feel for her.

She had to be sensible.

It was best she went back home and waited for Houdini to return.

∼

But Olivia began to get nervous when morning turned into afternoon then afternoon made its soft slide into evening. She paced in her flip flops, trying to convince herself everything would be fine.

Until she couldn't wait any longer. She went to grab her keys then stopped when someone knocked on the front door.

She froze. She wasn't expecting a delivery.

Someone rang the doorbell then knocked again.

Olivia opened it.

A tall, broad shouldered man stood there. Built like a mountain that would have a warning sign at its base: Approach with caution.

He had a jaw carved out of granite and guarded dark eyes, a mouth as thin as a razor blade and brown skin like brushed velvet.

She knew him from somewhere but couldn't quite place him.

She expected him to scold her, to let loose some expletives telling her how irresponsible she was. She steeled herself for the onslaught.

She swallowed and took a deep breath, whatever he had to say she was ready.

"Hello."

One word. That's all he said, and suddenly she was in a forest and there was a voice. That voice, in that tone, in that way. And his face, that face, it was *his face*! But that was impossible!

Olivia slammed the door shut before she could think. She didn't even know why the sound of his voice would elicit such a reaction. It made no sense and it was rude. And she was never rude. She was always polite. Manners, good manners, had been drilled into her since she'd been a child and here she'd lost a dog and slammed a door in a man's face. What was wrong with her?

She took a deep breath and opened the door.

"Sorry about that," she said with a light laugh, which she hoped didn't sound like the tail end of hysteria (or panic), "Um... A fly was about to get in."

"Right," the man said and he didn't sound annoyed, or doubtful or even very interested. He sounded bored. "I thought you might want this back."

Olivia wasn't quite sure what 'this' was, until she followed the man's gaze to the ground and saw a dog with a silly grin on its face.

Olivia fell to her knees with gratitude. "You naughty girl," she said, burying her face in the dog's fur. "I don't know how you did it." She glanced up at the solemn faced man. "Thank you."

He glanced away, looked uncomfortable. She noticed the mud on his jeans and shoes, the cut on his hand. Did he have to race after Daisy? Olivia felt her guilt grow.

She cleared her throat. "Where was she?"

"Just wandering."

"I don't know how to thank you."

He rubbed the back of his neck. "It's nothing."

"But it's the second time, right?"

"Second time?"

"That you've had to return her."

He paused, startled, then said, "Oh, right...yeah. It's fine."

She felt as if there was something he wasn't telling her but she didn't want to push him.

"I should go." He turned and headed down the steps.

Olivia quickly led Daisy inside and firmly closed the front door before she turned and raced after the stranger.

"Wait," she said, but she wasn't used to running in flip flops and she lost her balance.

She didn't know what alerted him first, her cry of alarm or the sound of her flip flop slipping off her foot, but the man quickly turned and caught her arm before she fell. "Careful."

She froze. He'd said those words to her before, in the exact same way. Was this some strange form of déjà vu? But it felt as if it had really happened before, in a dream. Except the day wasn't bright, his eyes hadn't met hers this close before. It had been too hazy for her to see them clearly. In her dreams his eyes were just dark. Now she could see they were a toasted walnut color.

He quickly withdrew as if sensing her unease. Why did she get the sense he was studying her?

Olivia was used to a man's gaze, but his was intense, as if he was trying to see deeper into her, past the beauty. As if he thought there was more to find. She inwardly laughed, he'd be disappointed. She didn't have a deep inner world, spent most of her time wondering how she'd be a help to others, never considering her own hopes and dreams, which were pretty simple, marriage and children, a home, family. Plus, a few dinner parties, family holidays, a lake house.

"What is it?" he said.

Her mind was blank. She didn't know whether to blame his voice or his eyes, but something about him made all rational thought disappear. Why had she raced after him again?

He sighed. "I really have to—"

"What's your name?"

"I live next door."

"That's not what I asked you."

"I know." He turned.

She rushed forward, hopping on one foot. "Can I treat you to lunch?" The words came out before she could stop them and they surprised her as much as they seemed to surprise him. She'd never asked a man out before, never had to. She always waited, but this time she felt like taking the lead. She wanted to not only thank him but find out more about him. That also wasn't like her. While she was interested in men, she'd never found men particularly interesting. She'd never had the need to. Her father was a prime example: Kind and dutiful but most importantly well-off. He provided for his family and left everything to the care of her mother. He seemed fine with that.

Olivia loved her father but didn't know him. Her mother didn't seem to know him either (he'd once surprised her mother with the knowledge that he'd had two dogs—-both boxers—-as a child, and that he liked the smell of limes) since knowing who her husband was as a person was very low on her list.

Her parents seemed happy. There was a genuine affection and that's all Olivia thought she could hope for. Her two sisters had also married well. Meaning their spouses would make sure they lived in the culture and class they'd been raised in and grown accustomed to.

But her Clifton cousins shook her.

Their pairings seemed to go deeper than checking off social boxes and societal expectations. They actually seemed to *like* their husbands. As if they'd have them as friends.

It was a foreign concept but one that intrigued her. Could a man be interesting? She didn't expect much. One lunch wouldn't go very far, but she was curious...

"Um..." His gaze had shifted away. He was going to turn her down, the thought shocked her. Irritated her a little if she were being honest. Why would he say no? "It's nothing more than lunch," she said quickly.

A quick smile came and went, "I know," he said.

"Then why were you going to turn me down?"

His gaze briefly met hers before it darted away again. "Who said I was going to turn you down?"

"You hesitated."

"Yes."

"Why?"

"Because that's what I do," he said with a tired sigh. He studied her for a long moment, folded his arms then said, "When?"

"Are you free today?"

"No."

She waited for him to expand, to offer a more suitable time, but when he didn't Olivia said, "Tomorrow?"

He rubbed the back of his neck, sighed as if contemplating the state of the world and all its ills before he nodded. "Tomorrow would work."

She felt oddly triumphant. "Great." She told him a restaurant she liked to frequent and the time they should meet.

He nodded and then turned and the motion again reminded her of a dream sequence.

"You still haven't told me your name," she said.

"I know."

Why the mystery? "What if I want to get in touch with you?"

"Like I said, I'm next door."

"But what if you can't make it?"

Another quick smile came and went. "Don't worry," he said. "I'll be there."

CHAPTER EIGHT

He was early.

But so was she, by at least ten minutes, even though it had taken her nearly an hour to look like she hadn't made an effort. She wore carefully applied makeup, a long braid that hung over her left shoulder and a cream colored summer dress with matching handbag and sandals.

But he'd arrived before her. She hadn't expected that.

She'd expected him to saunter into the restaurant maybe five to ten minutes late as if he didn't have a care in the world.

That wasn't the man she saw. He was a man dressed in dark trousers and a light shirt, well fitted. Didn't seem the type to use a tailor but his clothes didn't hang or bunch at odd angles. The mountain knew how to dress.

He didn't look nervous, but Olivia had a sense he was on edge.

She walked up to him and said in a teasing tone, "Are you married?"

He blinked. "No. Why?"

"You look like someone about to embark on an affair."

To her surprise he smiled. The appearance quick, sheepish, and mischievous before it disappeared like a shadow. "Sorry, no it's...it's been awhile since I've been out with someone."

"I'm glad to break the dry spell. So, what's your name?"

He stared at her shocked. "You still don't know?"

"Should I?" Was he a celebrity or something?

"I thought I gave you enough clues to figure it out."

"How would I figure it out?"

"I told you I live next door. It's pretty easy to get someone's name from that."

She felt like a prized idiot. Of course! She'd never thought to look him up. She wasn't used to having to work for anything. People usually told her about themselves willingly. She'd never had to make an effort. Why hadn't she thought to check? He must think she was every stereotype out there: A beauty with no brains. Perhaps he was right. No wonder he'd hesitated accepting a lunch date with her.

"Garrett." He held out his fist, when she looked at it in question he said, "I don't shake hands."

"Oh, I'm Olivia," she said awkwardly hitting his fist with her own. "I'm sorry."

"For what? Having better things to do than look me up? That's fine."

But it wasn't fine and Olivia mulled over her faux pas as she looked over the menu. It took her only seconds to realize he wasn't looking at his. He looked bored—again.

"You already know what you want?" she asked him.

"I checked the menu online."

"I see." He was efficient, she'd give him that. He was nothing like her previous date who'd spent nearly ten minutes figuring out what type of fizzy drink he preferred. Another date had taken nearly twenty minutes to decide what to order. She'd been starving that evening but thought it bad manners to order and eat when he was still undecided. Clearly Garrett wasn't like that.

The Mediterranean-inspired restaurant was better known for its name than its dishes. Years ago it had been a cutting edge destination for remarkable food, but had settled into satisfying average tastes and not offending anyone. So while the food would never disappoint, it was also quickly forgotten. She had chosen it precisely because it was safe and dependable and yet important enough to be noteworthy.

She wondered if he wanted to make the outing with her as short as possible. The thought made her heart sink.

It sank to her knees when the waiter arrived and Garrett said he'd like the salad then handed over the menu.

"Just a salad?" Olivia said after the waiter had taken her order. "As a starter?"

"No, the full meal."

She looked him over. He wasn't fat. It would be bad manners to ask if he was on a diet. But she was curious. She'd never see him again, and she was paying for this experience so she might as well get some answers.

"You didn't have to say yes, you know."

"I know that."

"Then why a salad?"

"Why not?"

"It's not filling and a man like you could finish it in four bites."

"A man like me?"

"A big man."

He nodded. "So that means I shove food in my mouth, talk with my mouth full, and probably eat with my hands?"

"No," she said suddenly flustered. "I didn't mean it like that. I just...it's a salad...it isn't the kind of food you...um... well..." She paused, hating how halting and awkward she sounded, so she finished in a rush, "It's not a meal you choose if you want to spend time with someone." Even to her own ears her words sounded ridiculous, but it was the best way she could explain herself.

Garrett leaned back. "Ahh...you think my food choice is a reflection on you? Are you really that vain?"

Olivia sipped her water. Best not to answer. And holding the glass kept her hand from gripping into a fist.

He sighed. "Sorry, that wasn't fair."

"I'm sorry too."

"That you invited me?"

"No, that from your viewpoint I'm a vain idiot."

He shook his head. "I never said you were an idiot."

"But you thought it."

He pointed at her. "That's a bad habit of yours."

"What?"

"Trying to read minds."

He was right. She didn't know him and she was trying to pretend that she did. That she could safely put him in a slot. That's how she was used to dealing with the world. Her mother had taught her the importance of anticipating other people's needs. To be two steps ahead. Even worse, she'd thought he'd be a little like the man in her dreams.

There had seemed to be a connection there, but reality

was painfully different. She should have left him alone. She should have waited for him to approach her instead of the other way round. That was what was wrong. She should have followed the well-trodden path. She shouldn't have acted out of character.

"And that's even worse," Olivia heard him say.

"Worse?"

"You second guess yourself."

He knew too much. Why did it feel as if he knew her so well? Being with him felt both familiar and awkward at the same time. Olivia couldn't make sense of it.

But she hated being a disappointment, best to bow out gracefully. "I'm so sorry I've wasted your time," she said. "It's still early and our food hasn't arrived yet, so we don't have to pretend that this isn't already a disaster."

His brows shot up. "And you came to this conclusion all because I ordered a salad?"

She almost laughed, could he make her sound anymore ridiculous? She smoothed the napkin on her lap, wanting to run. She'd never been with someone who kept making her feel as if she were petty and stupid.

"I like salads," Garrett said. "That's it. It's that simple." He studied her for a moment as if he sensed she didn't believe him then added, "The truth is I like the dressing. I know it's weird but it's the truth. I like salad dressing in all different forms. Some people are into wines, I'm into dressings. I like the different pairings, a garden salad versus a Caesar salad. The right dressing that blends well with feta cheese versus shredded American. I wonder when to use a classic vinaigrette or honey mustard. French or Italian?"

"You're serious?"

He nodded.

"You make a cheap date."

"I thought this wasn't a date."

"It isn't," Olivia said quickly, "I'm just making an observation."

"Still think it's a disaster?"

"I might have been a bit overdramatic."

Garrett held up his thumb and forefinger the space of a thimble. "Just a bit."

She smiled.

He nodded, pleased. "That's better."

When their food arrived at the table, without much fanfare from a waiter who seemed to care more about speed than grace as he plopped their dishes in front of them with a careless thud, Olivia watched as Garrett carefully drizzled a cholesterol laden, white stream of Ranch dressing (wanton caloric suicide) over a perfectly fine bed of mixed lettuce. He then lifted his fork and took delight in the first bite.

She held back a frown. She couldn't understand someone taking pleasure in basically spreading flavored mayonnaise on one's food. Dressings should be light, preferable transparent, not opaque and smothering.

But he didn't seem to care about the unsightly mess he'd created of his meal.

She watched him stab another forkful of food—sliced chicken, cherry tomato, romaine lettuce covered in white goo —and then waited. Because waiting was what she'd been brought up to do. Most men took any opportunity to talk about themselves and she'd learned to give them ample opportunity.

She waited for him to tell her when his love of salad

dressing began. She waited for him to tell her how and where he'd found Houdini. She'd waited for him to tell her something—-*anything*—-about himself, but he seemed in no hurry to.

He casually ate his salad and looked around the restaurant as if he didn't want to be anywhere else. It was strangely comforting.

And also strange. He didn't look at her. Ask questions. Was this really only a free lunch to him? Why did the thought depress her? It wasn't as if this was meant to lead to anything.

And yet...

He sipped his strawberry-lemonade. "So what do you do—?"

"I'm a—"

"For fun," he finished.

Olivia blinked. "For fun?"

He nodded.

She wasn't sure anyone had ever asked her that before. She didn't know how to reply. She felt like an actor on stage who'd suddenly found themselves in the wrong play.

"I don't know."

He frowned. "You don't have fun?"

"I-I like to shop."

"What do you buy?"

"Are you making fun of me?"

"Why would I make fun of you?"

"This is a serious question?"

"Yes. Why wouldn't it be?"

Olivia lowered her gaze to her plate and pushed her brown rice around with her fork, imagining her mother berating her for 'playing with her food'. But he'd given her a question she'd never anticipated and she had to find the correct reply. "I...um...like buying clothes and jewelry." That seemed harmless enough.

He looked at her for a long moment before he said, "I see," and returned to his salad.

What was that supposed to mean? "What do you do for fun?"

He stabbed at his salad. "It's been awhile, but I used to like axe-throwing."

"Oh."

His eyes danced with amusement. "Too lowbrow for you?"

She felt her cheeks heat, he wasn't far from wrong. It wasn't the kind of hobby people in her circle would understand.

The amusement faded as his gaze grew more serious when he said, "I also enjoy having lunch in the company of a beautiful woman."

She'd been called beautiful before, but the way he said it actually made heat steel into her cheeks, as if he found her beautiful in a way no one ever had before.

Somehow his voice was different here, softer, gentler.

Soon his salad would be finished and they'd have to part and she still didn't know much about him.

"What do you do for a living?" she asked him.

His gaze darted to her face then away again and she sensed a slight disappointment, which made her heart constrict, even though she didn't know why.

"I'm a nurse," he said in a flat voice. "Emergency."

Why not a doctor? she could hear her mother say. Was he

not ambitious enough? Bright enough? Then she hated herself for even thinking those things. At least he had a profession, she couldn't say the same.

Garrett sat back, keeping his gaze on the table. "Well, this has been great. I won't take up anymore of your time."

"You haven't finished your salad."

He sighed. "I thought I could, but I can't."

"I knew you'd put too much dressing on it," Olivia said with a smug grin. "It's an easy fix, just scrape some off and..." Her words trailed away as he shook his head.

"I'm not talking about the salad."

"You're not?"

His gaze met and held hers. "No, I mean I can't do *this*."

"I don't understand."

He pointed to her then himself. "This back and forth. I'm too tired for the mating game, the coupling game or whatever you call it. It's not a date, but you're still sizing me up: Does he have the right credentials? What will my friends think? What will my mother say? And I'm not in the mood or on the market—"

Alarm bells started to ring. He'd lied! "You *are* married?"

"For this," he finished.

"Oh." She hated how accurate he was. She felt ashamed. She'd convinced herself she'd asked him out because she wanted to thank him and know more about him, but she'd weighed and rated his every word and gesture against an invisible bar. He had every right to not want to see her again. She was shallow. She was becoming her mother. Her mother's voice had suddenly drowned out her own. She'd begun to see everything in life through that distorted filter: Worthy or unworthy.

"I'm sorry," Olivia said, each word feeling like a confession.

Garrett shrugged, let his gaze and voice fall. "Nothing to apologize for."

"Can we do this again?"

He began to shake his head. She reached out and covered his hand. "Please?"

His gaze met hers—a little tired, a little sad—before it darted away with the speed of a dragonfly. "No."

She withdrew her hand, biting back the bitter taste of disappointment. She'd made a mistake. She'd been dishonest. And he'd seen through her, saw that she had nothing to offer him except a pretty smile and false, light conversations. She didn't blame him for not wanting to see her again.

Olivia smiled and pretended it didn't hurt. She pretended that she wasn't devastated and humiliated and filled with regret. Garrett took her proffered smile, but instead of offering his own he sent her one of his guarded, mysterious looks and said, "Thanks."

She watched him leave and prayed that she didn't dream of him that night.

CHAPTER NINE

Of course she did.

In the dreamscape she always sensed him more than saw him. His shadow appeared first then his voice.

"You're quiet tonight," he said.

"I'm ashamed of myself. I met someone and I ruined it because I'm a rotten person."

"You're not rotten."

"He thinks so."

"You don't know that."

"You should have seen his face."

"You're mindreading again."

She gasped. "He said that too. You're so much alike and yet complete opposites. I don't know why you have his face or perhaps he has yours."

"This is only a dream."

"But it feels as if I'm going to lose you. That this may be our last night together."

He didn't reply.

Why wouldn't he reply?

"I don't want to lose you," Olivia said, urgent. "Please. Tell me I'm wrong."

She felt warm fingers on her bare arms. It was the first time she realized she was cold.

"Go back home," he said.

"No, not until you promise me—"

He kissed away her words.

Then disappeared.

IN THE GLARINGLY HARSH DAYLIGHT, when Olivia saw Garrett again nearly a week later (a moving mountain amid the bustle of the local farmer's market midday crowd), she thought she'd recoil. She thought she'd want to run away or hide behind one of the many stands where people were selling locally grown fruits, vegetables, and handicrafts. It would also be easy to hide behind the long brick community center building that hosted the outdoor market. The center set up the market on its grassy expanse of land from late spring to early autumn.

But Olivia didn't run or hide. She kept walking towards the man in dark jeans and formfitting orange T-shirt. Something drew her to him. Something *kept* drawing her to him. The voice in her head told her to stay away, but it took a moment to realize it was her mother's voice and not her own.

The voice told her all the reasons to reject him. There was no prestige in being a nurse's wife. She was meant for grander things.

But somehow, Garrett seemed right, because she sensed

he saw her and didn't care about those things. And she, deep in her heart, didn't want to care about those things either.

You're trying to rebel against me, her mother's voice said.

Perhaps that was true, but it also wasn't.

He'll never accept you. All you have is a pretty face.

That made her pause. This time it wasn't just her mother's voice, but her own. He hadn't wanted to finish lunch with her. He found her shallow, stupid, petty. She was only hurting herself trying to connect with him. But she wanted another chance to prove she wasn't those things, that she could be better. Do better.

She felt an urgent need to fix things. That if she couldn't do something in her real life the dreams that had given her comfort would be out of reach forever. Her dreams—-as strange and wild and unreal as they were—-made life bearable, gave her sanctuary, she couldn't lose them.

She rushed up to him. "Hi, I didn't expect to meet you —" Her words stopped on the end of a gasp when he turned around.

Gone was the man she'd only seen a couple of days ago. This man looked battle worn and exhausted. He carried three bulging cloth bags, but she couldn't tell what was inside them. She instinctively reached for him to offer him support but quickly drew her hand away before she touched him. "Did you have a bad night at the hospital?"

"No," he said. One word with no explanation, but it seemed to carry the weight of a thousand emotions. He began to turn, an effective way to close her off.

She grabbed his arm. "How can I help you?"

She felt his muscles tense, became aware of how big he was compared to her and she realized he was more solidly built than she'd expected him to be. Her hand looked like the size of a child's against his forearm, but he didn't pull away. He blinked quickly, like someone hit with a bright light after being in darkness for a long time. "W-why would you want to help me?"

Olivia swallowed, gaining courage. He could easily escape her grasp, but he hadn't. That meant something. "Because you look like you're going to collapse face first and..." She let her words fall away as well as her hand on his arm. It fell helplessly to her side.

"And what?"

"I like you."

The truth of her words both surprised and embarrassed her. But she had no desire to run away from them, deny them, pretend they didn't matter. Instead she welcomed this strange new feeling of truly being honest with herself and someone else.

Garrett didn't move. His jaw tensed, his hand tightened into a fist, he briefly closed his eyes and said her name, Olivia, and she heard a plea, a command, a wish, a vow. The voice of the forest called to her, seduced her, claimed her. She no longer felt the heat of the sun but rather the touch of a silent breeze, smelled the faint scent of strawberry licorice, and heard the ragged, stilted breathing of a man in pain. Did she really repel him that much?

She lightly touched the sleeve of his T-shirt. "Give me another chance. Please. I know you don't like me—"

His eyes met hers, dark like a night storm. "You don't know that."

"But—"

"I like you."

She stared, too stunned to reply.

He placed one of the bags on the ground, the tips of purple and orange carrots peeked out. He ran a tired hand down his face. "I didn't sleep well, that's all. Don't worry about it." He lifted the bag and turned.

What? What! He liked her? Then why hadn't he wanted to see her again? And why was he walking away as if what he'd told her didn't completely shake up her world? Was he toying with her feelings? Had she misheard him?

Before he completely disappeared into the crowd Olivia gathered herself and raced after him. "Garrett, wait!"

He continued walking.

Breathless she finally caught up with him. "I told you to wait."

He kept his gaze ahead and didn't slow his pace. "I didn't hear you."

"Did you drive here?"

"No, I walked."

Olivia stared at him surprised as she thought of how far their neighborhood was from the market. "No wonder you're exhausted. It's at least a five mile walk from your house."

Garrett shrugged. "I like to walk."

"And now you have all these bags."

He glanced down and nodded.

"Can I drive you home?"

She anticipated him refusing her and she came up with three ways she'd counter him but before she could come up with a fourth, he handed her one of his loaded bags and said, "Sure."

CHAPTER TEN

Olivia felt as if Garrett had handed her a bag filled with cement bricks. How could anything from a farmer's market weigh so much?

She was too polite to look inside the bag (or ask him to tell her) although she desperately wanted to. Garrett had made the bag look light when he'd held it out to her, but she'd had to use two hands to carry it. However, she did so cheerfully since she felt too triumphant to complain.

He'd accepted her help.

That was a win. He was silent—stayed silent the entire walk to her car—but it was still a win. He hadn't turned her down.

Her mood remained buoyant even as Garrett sat in the passenger seat with his eyes closed. When she saw the street that would lead them home, she decided to take another route. If he'd had trouble sleeping perhaps a few extra minutes wouldn't hurt.

And she thought about her dreams.

Why he—or rather someone like him—had been in them more than once again and again even though she'd never met him before.

"Have we reached New Jersey yet?" a deep voice said.

Olivia turned sharply to him. He still had his eyes closed. "I thought you were asleep."

"And I thought you were driving us home."

"I was—am—but I thought I'd take a longer route so that you could sleep."

Garrett took a deep breath and bit his lip before he said, "We can go home now."

"Did you sleep even a little?"

He opened his eyes and sat up. "You don't have to worry about me."

But I do and I don't know why.

With a soft sigh Olivia turned the car and headed towards home feeling disappointed and a little dejected. He hadn't even thanked her for the effort, not that it had worked and—

"It was a nice drive," he said staring out the passenger window. "Relaxing."

"I'm glad."

"And you didn't imagine it."

"Imagine?"

"What I said."

"About salad dressing?" she said, deliberately misunderstanding him.

To her surprise he laughed: a warm wonderful sound. "Yes, about salad dressing."

"I had wondered." She sent him a teasing look. "I wasn't sure."

He flashed her a sexy smile that made it clear he was no longer talking about salad dressing and said, "Well, wonder no more."

Olivia gripped the steering wheel, her heart picking up speed. She had wondered. But he still left her with so many questions.

Soon they were pulling into her driveway and she knew they would part.

She put the car in park and dashed out before he opened the door. She lifted the trunk and took out one of his bags before he could stop her then hurried over to his house.

Garrett looked amused but didn't say anything as he passed her and walked up the porch steps to his front door.

She followed behind. She felt as if this was a critical opportunity but she didn't know what to do.

She watched him open the door and she told him to rest well. She didn't know why she touched his sleeve, but he turned to her in surprise and his gaze captured hers with a flicker of desire that startled her.

For a brief moment he didn't look tired or worn he looked— hungry.

Desire she was used to, but not desire like this. Desire tempered and tamed. Why? Why did he fight his attraction to her? Shyness? Fear? What was holding him back?

She took a risk. She stepped forward. "I dream about you."

The flickering flame in his penetrating gaze shifted to a smoldering fire. But he still took a step back, eager to keep a distance she didn't want to give him. She dropped the bag, pulled him down towards her and pressed her lips against his. She steeled herself to feel his hands on her shoulders as he shoved her back. She prepared herself to be pushed away, which he did. Shoving her inside and closing the door before wrapping his arms around her.

He whispered something against her lips, a plea, a command— she wasn't sure—before his lips met hers.

A scorching kiss tinged with pent up longing, sent her spinning. His hot hands, sliding down her back, stoking a fire within her, his hard body pressed against hers, revealing a desire as fierce as her own. They fell on the couch where he deepened the kiss to one of pure ecstasy, his roving hands making their way under her blouse in a smooth, hot exploration. Reality proved better than any dream. She'd never imagined passion could feel like this.

She heard him softly swear before he abruptly stood. "I have to put the groceries away," he said.

Olivia stared at him surprised, her lips still burning, her skin tingling from everywhere he'd touched her. His words confused her, but she didn't want to overthink them. "Let me help..." She began but Garrett was shaking his head and picking up the bags.

"I'll be back in a minute," he said.

She didn't know what had happened. Why he'd shifted again and closed her off. She wondered if she should leave but then Garrett paused, looked at her with a gleam of intent and added, "I promise."

CHAPTER ELEVEN

Have we met? Garrett had skirted the question because he couldn't tell Olivia the truth. She might not believe him. And it seemed odd. He didn't want to frighten her. And in a way they hadn't really met. Not in a normal sense.

But if she knew the truth would she forgive him?

Garrett put his items away—the apples and cherries in the cupboard and the potatoes in the fridge until he realized his error and switched them—wondering what to do next. He'd bought more items than he needed, plus some items that he didn't need (like ten bars of handmade soap: five that looked like a loaf of lemon poppy seed cake, three that smelled like cinnamon cocoa and two that held a citrus blend). The shopping trip had been an impulsive decision and he certainly hadn't planned on seeing Olivia there. Or letting her drive him home.

Or letting her kiss him.

Or letting her into his house and nearly taking her on the sofa.

Garrett took a deep steadying breath and slowly closed the cupboard.

He couldn't turn back now. Didn't want to. Having her here was worth the risk.

She didn't have to know. There were so many things he was not saying, but it felt better this way. He'd be patient, take his time, she didn't have to know anything yet. He'd not allowed himself to hope like this in a long time. He'd felt weary, dejected. She made him feel part of the world again. As if he could matter to someone. Feel fully human again.

He returned to the living room and sat beside Olivia making her feel safe. Unlike her friend's sofa, Olivia sank into the soft, comfortable cushions of Garrett's dark blue cotton sofa with a grin.

He had returned as he'd promised. She hadn't made a mistake and then he spoke to her in that voice. That same voice from the dark path of her dreams where he spoke in a luring voice sweet with promise, "Tell me about these dreams," he said.

She opened her mouth but no words spilled out. She thought it would be easy to talk about them, especially with him listening so intently but somehow his invitation had left her mute. She realized she didn't want to talk, that talking seemed like it would break a spell. There were some things best left unsaid, some experiences better left to the dreamscape.

Garrett seemed to sense her hesitation and his gaze drifted away, but she didn't want that. She covered his hand and said, "Do you dream about me?"

He paused, carefully choosing his words. "You are like a dream to me."

It was a strange statement, but perhaps, like her, he didn't want to go into detail. It was too strange to think one could dream about a stranger, to have a special, seemingly unearthly, connection.

She stood and held out her hand. "Let's make this real."

He took her hand and led her to the bedroom then said, "Give me five minutes," before he disappeared into the bathroom and she heard the shower turn on. She smiled. He didn't have to do that but she appreciated the effort.

She stripped out of her khaki trousers and green blouse and was about to take off her bra when she noticed the closet door partially open. She walked over to close it then stopped when she noticed a box on the ground with items spilling out of it. She crept closer and recognized one of the items: Her scarf.

Then she saw more: Her missing socks, the earrings, the bracelet. What were they doing here?

Was this why he'd felt familiar? He'd been in her bedroom? Had he looked over her while she was sleeping and that's why his scent had felt familiar? He'd been in her house, in her room!

She frantically changed. She'd been wrong about him. So desperately wrong.

Garrett came out of the bathroom, a towel wrapped around his waist, and noticed her fully dressed. He frowned confused and said, "What's—" before he glanced at the open closet and swore. "I can explain."

He saw her eyes widen with fear and followed her gaze to his neck—where he wore a necklace with a crescent moon and an amethyst stone perched in the curve of it. He'd forgotten to take it off. He should have been more careful. He swore again. "No, it's not...Please. Let me—"

"I don't want to hear it," Olivia half shouted, half screamed. This was worse than she could have imagined.

"Please Olivia. It's not what you think."

She pointed at him with a trembling hand. "That's my necklace." She pointed towards the closet. "Those are my things. You were in my house!"

He took a step towards her, his hands held up in surrender and firmly said, "I was never in your house."

She stepped back, ready to strike him if she had to, surveying his large form for vulnerable places that would do the most damage and allow her to escape. "Then how did you get these things?"

"Just let me—"

"No." She covered her ears. He'd lie and she wasn't in the mood for more lies. Her life had been filled with them. She'd made the worst mistake in her life.

She turned and raced out of the room, down the stairs, out the front door. He didn't stop her. He could have, but he didn't.

Once home, Olivia slammed the front door closed and locked the top bolt. Lungs burning, tears stinging, she gripped her hands into fists.

Lies. Lies. Lies. She'd deluded herself. There hadn't been an otherworldly connection, just a pervert with a sexy smile.

Moments later Garrett knocked—not pounded—knocked like a gentleman (as if he wasn't a monster) and said in a calm, gentle voice, "I know this looks bad, but it's not what you think. Truly."

Olivia gritted her teeth. It was probably the same tone he used with patients.

"I don't want to frighten you," he continued in the same soothing, reasonable voice that almost made her want to listen to him and hear what he had to say, "so I'll give you space. When you're ready, please let me talk to you."

Olivia squeezed her eyes shut, but the tears still fell. She'd never be ready. She'd never trust again.

She didn't dare sleep that night.

The following morning, while making her way through breakfast—a slice of toast with orange marmalade that she ate like a mouse nibbling cheese—the alarm on her phone went off. She looked at the notice and swore. The luncheon! It was today! Her mother was going to introduce her to another blind date.

Olivia quickly checked her reflection in the bathroom mirror. At least she hadn't cried so there was no damage to repair to her eyes and nose. She looked a little drawn because she hadn't slept. Makeup would cover that up.

"You look tired," her mother said with a frown (that only emphasized her long, aquiline nose and thick heavy eyebrows) when she met Olivia outside the Brazilian restaurant, the savory scent of *pão de queijo* (cheese bread) wafting through the front doors.

"I'm fine," Olivia lied. "I tried a new foundation that I realized, too late, didn't work with my skin tone." She lowered her gaze looking properly dismayed and because she knew how to lie convincingly her mother didn't question her.

Her mother made an unnecessary, but showy, introduction between Olivia and her date then discreetly disappeared. But not before sending Olivia a warning glance that said her chances of a good match were dwindling and that she better not mess this up.

Fifteen minutes later Olivia realized there was nothing overtly wrong with the man. It was her. She realized it had always been her. Part of her didn't want this.

She laughed at jokes that were more corny than funny (someone else would probably find them hilarious), nodded as if interested in the essential role of worms in a successful garden and the beauty of biophysics, subjects that fascinated him and bored her (someone else would appreciate these interests more), and he didn't ask her many questions about herself. Few did. She always had rote replies for the standard set and only needed two of them this time: Yes, I am enjoying myself, thank you so much for asking. Yes, I find summer especially hot this year.

Only Garrett had thrown her off balance with his probing gaze and strange questions.

But she wouldn't think about him.

Even though he'd ruined her chance at happiness.

She couldn't do this game anymore. It didn't suit her. She didn't trust herself. Trust her judgment.

Perhaps that's why lies were better than truths. You knew better than to trust them. If she hadn't stopped lying to herself, if she hadn't tried to be completely herself, she wouldn't have had her heart broken.

CHAPTER TWELVE

Garrett sat in the moonlit garden and waited for a woman who wouldn't show. It was the second night in a row.

He knew Olivia wouldn't come, but that didn't stop him from sitting in one of the wrought iron chairs and drumming his hand against the table.

He'd lost her trust. He wished he'd handled things better even though he still wasn't sure how he could have handled it any differently. If he'd shown her the items sooner, he wouldn't have gotten a chance to have lunch with her, to walk with her. He wouldn't have allowed this wakeful dream to continue. And he'd selfishly wanted it to.

She'd approached him without pretense, accepted him. He knew that he wasn't what she'd want in real life. He didn't check off all the right boxes. Twice, when he could see her calculating his potential (appraising him like an antique dealer), he'd thought of showing her what she'd done, taking her down a peg, but then had decided against it.

He still didn't know why.

Perhaps because in spite of her snobbery there was someone sweet there, someone he wanted to know better. He wanted to know the woman who liked to dance, who brought him odd gifts. The sleepwalker had drawn him.

The first time she'd wandered into his unkempt garden, where he'd been sitting after another sleepless night, making his way through a tall, cold glass of strawberry milk, he was certain he had to be dreaming. He wasn't the kind of man who had beautiful women coming into his life on moonlit evenings. But he must be dreaming. The burnout had brought a lot of new sights and sensations he'd never had before. This vivid dream had to be one of them.

But it wasn't a dream he could understand. Why would a model attractive, honey skinned woman with long black hair end up in his garden? Dressed in a flimsy nightdress and clunky boots?

It took him only a few seconds to realize he was fully awake, but she was the one asleep. He tried to gently warn her away, but she only smiled.

She was the last thing he needed. Another problem. Someone who needed help. He looked at her with a jaded eye. Her beauty didn't affect him. He'd stopped even feeling awe at the sight of a starry sky or a waterfall.

He watched her as dispassionately as he would a ladybug landing on a rose with dewdrops that sparkled like diamonds. But then she did something strange. Something that hurt a little, shifting his cold heart with heat he hadn't wanted to feel, making it come alive again.

She gave him a raspberry colored silk scarf, draping it on

his shoulder, before spinning away and moving about the garden in a swaying, playful dance.

The scarf held the scent of jasmine and rose as he slid the soft, fragile fabric over his palm.

Then he watched her dance and sensed something lost and sad about her. That had been his downfall. If she hadn't been vulnerable, if it had been daytime he would have been able to shut his heart against her, but not at night, darkness hid too many dangers.

And this was a dangerous situation.

Wasn't this why he'd taken a break from the ER? He didn't need any more danger. He'd stayed holed up in his house to get away from even the slightest whiff of it. But the greatest danger of all was that he felt fear. He hadn't felt anything in months and yet, he felt anything but numb as the striking woman moved around his garden as if she belonged there.

He felt his heart race, his mouth felt dry.

Paralyzed, he watched her dance on the edge of danger in a strange man's garden, every inch of him screaming for him to save her as much as he wanted to stay away.

But he couldn't because she was vulnerable and he was a rescuer. He couldn't watch and not do anything. Although he should.

But the truth—though terrifying—was that she made him feel alive, filling the hollow parts of him with a renewed sense of purpose.

When she stopped dancing and started to go through his weed choked garden as if it were as beautiful as a field of fresh lavender, Garrett told her to return home.

To his relief she did. He gently led her, without touch,

only guiding her with his voice, back to her place, following her at a safe distance, both surprised and relieved that she was his next door neighbor.

He'd never seen her before. Then he vaguely remembered his chatty neighbor telling him about someone looking after her dog and house while she was on holiday.

But whether the woman was a house/dog sitter or someone else Garrett had no intention of seeing her again.

Unfortunately, she returned the following evening and offered him another item—earrings—and said a nonsense poem.

And although he had no use for the earrings, the offered item, like the one before it, felt like a gift rather than charity. She wasn't handing him things she no longer needed, her actions, or rather how he'd interpreted them, seemed to mean that she cared.

It was strange that he hadn't realized that was what he'd needed. The feeling of someone caring about him. He'd forgotten to care for himself. He hadn't asked for help, thinking he could shoulder the long hours, the stress, the strain of his job all on his own. Until he realized he couldn't.

Night after night she returned and he grew used to the nightly encounters.

He looked forward to them, never expecting that the ghastly hand of reality would strangle that sacred time with her. Nor would he have imagined reality would come in the form of a dog.

A small, shaggy dog he liked.

The dog ruined Garrett's carefully laid plan to keep the time with the sleepwalker limited to the evening hours.

In truth, it was his fault for forgetting about it.

He'd only noticed the dog the second time the sleep-walker had come to visit. The dog walked beside the dreamer, as he'd thought of her before he knew her name, careful not to bark or touch her. The dog trotted happily beside her as if nothing was wrong.

One evening, Garrett had led the dreamer home without thinking of the canine that had been with her. Until he returned to his garden and saw the dog sitting next to the iron table, smiling at him.

He swore. He couldn't return the dog now and wake her up.

He thought about doing nothing. The dog would soon get bored and find its way home. But the following day it seemed to be in no hurry to return home and Garrett could imagine the owner's panic.

By late morning he picked up the dog determined to hand it over, but once he turned the corner, he lost courage.

What would he say to her? He didn't want to answer any questions.

He returned home and feeling like a coward, waited until she left then put on a baseball cap to shield is face, in case he was captured on camera, hurried over and left the dog tied up, making sure it had plenty of shade, water and food.

He briefly considered also returning the scarf, earrings and other items with the dog, as if the dog had taken them, but he didn't want to get the dog in trouble or frighten the dreamer with the belief that some stranger had handled her precious things, so he'd kept them.

But that was only one reason.

He'd also kept them as treasures. Souvenirs of the

moments he'd shared with her. Each item he held onto felt as if he were capturing a piece of her he couldn't claim. The one he treasured most was the necklace—a crescent shaped moon and purple stone. It was one item he could wear, carefully concealed underneath his shirts, and think of her.

He never expected the dog would stay back a second time.

That night Garrett had been certain the dog had returned with the dreamer only to return home moments later to hear whimpering and scratching at his back door.

When he opened it, the dog trotted inside as if she'd been invited. Garrett couldn't figure out how it had managed its escape. Had the dog only pretended to go inside with the dreamer and then quickly dashed back out without him noticing, only to hide in the garden when he'd returned home?

It seemed too clever and devious, but he didn't put it past the smug faced canine. He picked it up and hurried next door. He placed the dog on the porch and quietly commanded it to stay.

The dog sneezed, but to his relief, didn't move.

Garrett took a cautious step back ready to leave when the lights on the main floor came on.

Oh no, was she awake? Had he made a sound? If she opened the door how would he explain himself? It was night. He was a stranger. He as a man. A big man at that. The sight of him would terrify her. But maybe she wouldn't open the door...

No, the door was opening!

Garrett leaped over the side of the porch and fell down hard on one of the bushes. He held his breath as the light from inside spilled onto the porch. At least she'd see the dog and that would be over. He swallowed as the triangle of light slowly faded as the door closed.

Then the porch fell into darkness once more. Garrett watched the light upstairs come on and then light on the main floor turned off.

He closed his eyes and released a long sigh. He was safe.

He opened his eyes and bit back a curse. He couldn't believe his eyes.

Sitting in front of him was the shaggy little dog. It must have followed him when he'd jumped over the side, thinking it was a game.

Garrett groaned and picked up the dog, admitting defeat.

He returned home and cleaned the cut on his hand, but didn't bother with the mud on his jeans and shoes. He tossed of his shoes and collapsed on the couch in defeat. The little dog happily joined him and promptly went to sleep.

The next day, Garrett considered waiting until the dreamer left home and returning the dog as he had before—completely unnoticed. But gnawing thoughts began to eat away at his conscience. What if one night the dreamer wandered into someone else's garden? Or down the street? Or worse, was lured into someone's car and never seen again?

He squeezed his eyes shut. He knew he was being overly dramatic, the likelihood of those scenarios happening was low, but he felt he had to do something.

With a string of curses, Garrett resigned himself to his fate. He had to face the dreamer in the daytime.

～

WHAT FIRST SHOCKED him when the dreamer opened the front door was how different she looked when awake. It was as though she were a twin with a different manner and personality. None of the elegant inhibition was there, none of the free, fresh fun in her features or the way she moved. Everything seemed calculated. Studied. Polished. Practiced.

He felt his heart fall, with any feelings for her slowly crumbling to dust.

They were both wide awake now and any chance of a relationship, no matter how simple, had been only a dream.

Then she'd slammed the door in his face.

The action had shocked him, but by the devastated look on her face when she opened the door, her actions had also shocked her. Garrett had to bite the inside of his cheek to keep himself from laughing at how flustered she looked as she lied about a bee or something.

Her halting words and fluttering lashes allowed him to look past the beautiful mask and see glimpses of the dreamer. The two personalities may be different but he still sensed something lost and sad about her.

But he was still determined to stay away. He meant to return the dog and that would be the end of it.

If only she hadn't raced after him (what possessed her to do that?) and nearly fallen (why was she wearing such clunky flip flops?) he could have safely walked away.

But when he grabbed her arm to keep her from falling, he saw a vulnerability, a longing within her when their eyes met and he dared to think he could fill it. It was a natural instinct for him to want to help, to want to heal, to stop someone else's suffering even it would cause his own. He felt it gave his life purpose.

GARRETT SIPPED his chilled strawberry milk, a habit he'd picked up during his sleepless nights, the moonlight catching the side of the glass as a drop of water slid down the side and fell on the table.

With a tinge of regret and a heap of defiance he remembered the moment he'd accepted the dreamer's invitation to lunch, curious to find out more about her. And he discovered beneath the snobbery, the calculated air of sophistication, she liked him and cared about him. He hadn't expected that.

He hadn't meant to fall in love with her.

But now none of that mattered. Burnout wasn't the reason he felt weary and empty.

He was back where he'd started. Alone at night in his weedy garden with only his thoughts to keep him company with no promise of the anticipated arrival of a little dog and a dreamer.

Garrett closed his eyes, knowing sleep wouldn't come.

CHAPTER THIRTEEN

The small cardboard box left on the porch came as a surprise.

Olivia tore off the note that had been taped to the top and read: *Here are your things. When you're ready to talk here is my number.*

She thought of ripping up the note and turning it into confetti.

But she didn't. She took the box inside and set it on the kitchen counter. She opened the box and peered inside but didn't touch anything. They seemed soiled somehow.

Why would he take such odd objects? Why would he look at her with such sincerity and say he'd never been in her house?

Why did she want to believe him?

Because the alternative was too painful, that's why. She hated the thought that she'd misread him and that he was not who she'd thought he was.

But although the box was half empty the sight of it filled her with questions.

Questions she needed answers to.

Olivia hurried outside and noticed that Garrett's silver Nissan was in the driveway, but that didn't mean he was at home. She knew that he liked to take long walks.

She pulled out her phone and texted him (because she didn't want to hear his voice) with the message: *Are you home?*

Before she turned to go back inside he responded with: *Yes.*

For a moment her hands shook, she steadied them then replied: *Meet me on the porch.*

It seemed like a safe choice. It was open, visible from the street and on her turf.

Olivia went inside and grabbed the box from the counter. When she opened the door to go back out, Daisy raced past her like a champion greyhound and happily greeted the slow moving mountain making its way up the path to her house.

She watched him with caution as an afternoon summer breeze toyed with the hem of his grey short-sleeved shirt, while carrying the scent of smoked vegetables from some-one's grill.

She saw no defeat in Garrett's steady gait, no drooped shoulders. He walked tall, without apology and the sight of his arrogance angered her until their eyes met.

It happened as he climbed the porch steps. Although no words passed between them, his penetrating gaze spoke to her very core. His dark brown eyes offered a quiet plea, a soft entreaty, and also, strangely, forgiveness, as if he were saying no matter what happened his feelings for her would never change.

Olivia found herself the first to look away. Not because he intimidated her but because he reminded her of how much she still cared.

Garrett sat down on one of the wooden chairs and gave Daisy another friendly pat before he clasped his hands together and waited.

She sat, set the box down between them, and folded her arms. "Okay, explain. Why did you have my things?"

"Because you gave them to me."

She blinked. "No, I didn't."

"Yes, you did."

Was this what gaslighting was about? He was trying to control her mind? Make her doubt herself?

"When you were sleep walking," he continued.

"Sleepwalking?"

He nodded.

"I was sleepwalking?"

He nodded again.

"But I don't—"

Garrett pulled out a phone from his back pocket and held it out to her. "I have a video of the second time. I didn't think you'd believe me."

She didn't. She still had a hard time believing her eyes when she saw a version of herself in a white nightdress and boots crossing into his garden and placing an object there. It explained how Houdini had escaped a locked house, she'd let the dog out. It explained the sometimes soreness of her limbs. It made no sense. She'd never done anything like this before. Why now? Why his place?

In the video she saw Garrett carefully approaching her. Although there was no sound she could imagine the voice he'd used with her, the soothing one she'd thought had originated from her dreams, but actually had come the other way round. From reality to dream.

She felt ashamed, embarrassed. She thought of his hesitation with her. Of course she wasn't someone he'd want to get involved with if she behaved like this.

Olivia watched in horror as the version of her on the tiny screen danced, she twirled and leaped. The movements weren't skilled, graceful, elegant. They were wild, untamed, uninhibited.

"I didn't know how to return the items without scaring you," he said. "There are many reasons people sleepwalk so don't feel bad about it."

She stared down at her hands. She noticed Daisy's shaggy head at the corner of her eye, and then felt the dog brush against her leg as if trying to offer comfort, but Olivia couldn't be comforted. She was mortified.

"There's no reason to be embarrassed," Garrett said. "You must have been under a lot of strain and this made you happy. You were always happy."

She thought of the wedding invitations on the kitchen counter and the disastrous blind dates and her mother's phone calls and her sense of feeling like a failure. This was how she dealt with it? By dancing wildly in a garden and giving away things?

She closed her eyes and said in a low voice, "Have you shown this to anyone else?"

"Why would I?"

She looked down at her hands. "For a laugh?"

"Olivia, look at me."

"No."

She heard him sigh. "I'd never laugh at you."

That didn't make her feel better.

"Relax, no one else has seen it so your reputation is safe."

"Oh."

"The truth is, after the first shock, I looked forward to you coming."

Olivia looked up at him, surprised. "Why?"

Garrett bit his lip then a boyish grin touched them. "Because it was fun. At the time, I had trouble sleeping but you made the night something I didn't dread anymore."

She thought of the items she'd given away, except for the earrings and bracelet, all the items were worn on the feet or around the neck. Did that mean anything, symbolize something?

He shrugged. "I didn't know what to do or say without frightening you and—"

She surged to her feet. "That's fine. You have returned them and I'm thankful. You can go now."

Garrett studied her for a long moment then softly said her name.

Suddenly, stretched out before her, she saw the path he was offering her and that path frightened her. Unlike in her dream she didn't feel as daring and bold in real life. It was easier to be with someone when it was better than being alone, when you were fulfilling a role, playing a part. It wasn't easy being imperfect and truly real with someone you genuinely liked and cared about. That felt too risky.

Something in her expression must have told him more than she'd wanted him to know because his gaze dimmed with disappointment and the sight of it crushed her. She hated feeling like a failure and a coward, although she feared she was both.

Olivia turned to the door and called out to the dog in a bright tone, which sounded false even to her own ears. "Come on Daisy."

"It's okay to be scared." Garrett paused, lowered his voice. "You know how I feel about you."

She opened the door, resisting the pull to turn to him and fall into his arms. "It's probably pity."

"Don't do that."

She spun around and faced him, fueled by her shame. "It's true. I'm not fun. I'm not interesting. You think I'm attractive, and my sleepwalking might make me an amusing novelty, but you'll grow bored of that after awhile."

"You're doing it again, trying to read my mind. You're so much more when you allow yourself to be real."

He was right. "I'm sorry. I'm...not ready."

Before she stepped inside Garrett said, "Wait."

Olivia turned to him in question and saw him removing something from his neck. "I keep forgetting to give this back to you." He held it out to her.

She saw a necklace with a silver chain and a crescent shaped moon, the afternoon light touching the purple hues of the amethyst stone settled in the curve of it.

The gemstone's healing properties seemed to whisper to her the power of its calm, restorative powers. The affect surprised her, she couldn't read stones and had no special abilities and yet...

She remembered her cousin Jessie once telling her that the amethyst was thought to protect one from nightmares and insomnia. It also could balance emotions and help those who wore it to stay calm in chaos.

Did her subconscious know that when she gave it to him? How did she know that he needed it?

She thought of reaching for it, but something made her recoil from taking it back. The pendant belonged to him now.

"Keep it," she said before she went inside and firmly closed the door.

CHAPTER FOURTEEN

He had no name. Not at first. Not one she wanted to use. Instead he appeared as a silhouette in the brittle moonlight, sitting alone in a quiet garden.

She made her way to him, the object in his hand taking the form of a glass filled with a creamy looking liquid.

The glass hit the table with a thud when he noticed her. The light metallic jingle of a dog's collar echoed in the still evening as Daisy happily trotted over to him.

He patted the dog, his gaze never leaving her face.

"I'm not asleep," Olivia said.

Garrett slowly rose to his feet. "I know."

"I tried but I couldn't sleep...not without you." She held out her hand.

He stared at it.

"I know you don't shake hands, but can you hold them?"

He lifted his heated gaze to her face and said in a velvet tone, "I want to hold more than your hand."

She took a step closer. "I was hoping you'd say that."

Garrett folded his arms. "What else where you hoping for?"

Olivia swallowed, uncertain. He wasn't reacting the way she'd hoped he would. But after the way she'd treated him that afternoon she couldn't blame him. She'd have to regain his trust. "I was hoping that you'd forgive me. That you'd give me another chance. That you'd tell me what I needed to do to—"

He pressed his finger against her mouth. "I only have one favor."

"What?"

He lifted something from the table and she noticed the silver chain and moon shaped pendant. He held it out to her. "Give this to me."

She almost recoiled again, shirking away from what he was asking her. *Prove to me how you really feel, offer me something for real.* It was a test.

Olivia steadied her shaking hands and took the necklace. She swallowed down the knot in her throat, and steeled herself against her thudding heart. Garrett humbly bowed his head so that she could put the necklace over his head and drape it around his neck. This time she would remember. It would always be a special moment between them.

With a satisfied smile she stared at the necklace. She'd taken the first crucial step. She didn't need to know all the answers. She only had to be real. "Now, what—?"

Her words ended with a gasp, when Garrett swept her into his arms and covered her mouth with his own.

Surprise quickly turned to pleasure as she surrendered to

the warmth of his strong embrace. The dark unknown no longer frightened her. She was filled with a giddy excitement.

Because the path she'd chosen led to an unassuming man who tasted like strawberries and sugar...and felt like home.

Your journey with Olivia and Garrett may have ended here, but if you're unfamiliar with her cousins—Jessie, Teresa and Michelle Clifton (and the men who shake up their worlds)— then a new adventure is about to begin.

Read on for a glimpse of how the Clifton Sisters series all began...

THE SAPPHIRE PENDANT

CHAPTER ONE

"For God's sake, Jessie, let's get out of here before we're caught," Wendy scolded in a harsh, loud whisper that seemed to bounce off the dark mahogany chairs and glass display cases in the room.

Jessie barely heard the warning, her cinnamon eyes fixed on a display case near the far wall. Its contents whispered to her in a soft, haunting song.

"I must get this back somehow," she muttered, staring at the sapphire pendant that lay seductively in its velvet bed.

Wendy grabbed her arm, eager to leave before either their boss or the owner, Mrs. Ashford, saw them. "So you've said many times." Her blues eyes shifted to the closed door, under which a sliver of light flickered as a shadow passed.

"I promised my father, when he sold it, that I would get it back one day." Jessie swallowed, trying to dislodge the tightness in her throat. Neither her father nor her mother had lived to see her fulfill that promise, but she would do it anyway.

"Well, if you don't have a job, you won't be able to afford it. Susan was looking for you."

Jessie's nagging thoughts quickly disappeared. "Damn." She couldn't afford to get fired again. Aside from having bills to pay, her eldest sister would kill her. She clicked off her penlight, pushed it into her trousers pocket, and headed for the door.

They raced towards the stairs. Jessie suddenly halted at the sight of a striking woman draped in a smoke-colored silk dress, her cunning dark eyes surveying the crowd from the top of the circular staircase.

She took a step back, ready to flee in the other direction. "We'll have to go around the back."

"Why?"

"Because that's Stephanie Radson. She works with Kenneth."

Wendy rested a hand on her hip. "So what?"

It meant he was lurking somewhere nearby, and Jessie always did her best to avoid him. "I want to go out back," she said hastily.

"That's too far."

"Fine, then I'll meet you in the kitchen."

Wendy only shook her head as they parted ways.

Jessie raced down the hall, then halted when she saw Amelia Wainwright, an older woman of indeterminate years, who had two buried husbands and a habit of talking without taking a breath. Jessie moved to duck into a room, but Amelia saw her and waved.

"Oh, good. I was hoping you would be here."

Jessie groaned, then plastered on a smile. "Yes, well—"

"I am so glad to have a moment with you, because I have

a question and I was thinking to myself, 'Who do I know that can help me find the answer?' And I racked my brain, and nothing came; I just couldn't readily think of anyone to help me. And then I thought about the last party I attended—I think it was three months ago?—and you did a reading there, saying that Mrs. Ostick would have a new arrival soon. Of course we all thought that finally her daughter was expecting, but instead her son got a divorce and had to move back home, but she did get that new arrival you were talking about. So I thought to myself, 'That's it! Jessie Clifton can help me!' And now here you are." She smiled.

Jessie glanced at her watch. "I'm on duty right now and I have to get back to the kitchen."

Amelia's smile began to fade, and a look of anxiety entered her hazel eyes. "Oh, but it's just a quick question. I won't take up too much of your time. I know how hectic working at a party like this can be. Well, I don't know personally, but I can imagine—"

Jessie shifted impatiently, but kept her voice gentle. "What is your question?"

Amelia glanced up, tapping her finger against her bottom lip. "When I woke up this morning, for some reason, I had to wear this bracelet." She held out her wrist. "I haven't worn this bracelet in years—ever since poor Christopher passed away. He gave it to me, you know. I—"

Jessie shoved her hands in her pockets and rocked on her heels, hoping the woman would get to the point soon. "And what do you want to know?"

"Why did I choose to wear it? What does that mean?"

Jessie sighed, then held out her hand. Amelia took off her bracelet and placed it in Jessie's palm. Jessie ran her fingers over the diamond-and-emerald bracelet, ignoring its cost to focus on its meaning. She let it rest in her hand a moment so that her intuition could read the energy there. She glanced up and read Amelia's face. Once she had gathered all the information she needed, she clasped the bracelet on Amelia's wrist. "You're worried about your health, aren't you?"

Amelia clutched her hands together and nodded, her hazel eyes glistening with unshed tears.

Jessie smiled reassuringly. "There is nothing to worry about. You're only experiencing indigestion. You do not have the same stomach cancer that killed your husband." She patted Amelia on the shoulder. "Now, I suggest you make an appointment with your doctor to put your mind at ease, and tell your cook to stop experimenting with her spice collection."

Amelia stretched out her arms. "How can I ever thank you enough?"

Jessie took a step back and waved the thanks away. "It's nothing, really. I'd better go." Before Amelia could say any more, Jessie rushed past her and hurried through the back door. She raced across the immaculate back lawns of the Ashford mansion like a gazelle running from a pack of hyenas.

She dodged a man carrying a table, jumped over a lady arranging flowers along the house, and slid to a stop in front of the servants' entrance. She adjusted her catering uniform and walked into the kitchen.

Wendy approached her with a paper towel. "Where have you been? You look like a melting chocolate sundae."

"Very funny," Jessie said, wiping the sweat sliding down her forehead. "I got cornered by Mrs. Wainwright." She tossed the towel away, envying her best friend's cool composure. Her olive-toned skin looked a bit flushed, but her black hair was pulled in a strict bun and her uniform was perfect, a lesson she'd learned from her French West Indian parents.

"Don't do that again," Wendy said, turning towards the ovens.

"I won't."

Susan, Montey's chief assistant, pointed at her. "Montey was looking for you," she warned, watching Jessie make her way around the kitchen. "I had to cover for you."

Jessie flashed a sheepish grin. "Sorry, I—"

"No time for excuses." Susan pointed to a carton of shrimp. "Put those in the fridge, then help Carole arrange the hors d'oeuvres." She raised her voice. "Make sure she doesn't eat any."

"I won't," Carole replied in a hurt tone.

Jessie put the carton in the fridge, then joined Carole, whose greedy fingers were reaching for a tantalizing miniature asparagus tart. Jessie slapped her hand away. "Those are for the guests."

"They won't miss just one," Carole argued, popping one in her mouth.

"Montey will notice."

Carole licked her long, slim fingers. Despite having the appetite of a polar bear, she had the figure of a model. Like many others in the Garden catering crew, she was saving money for school next year. "I'll say I dropped it."

"Then you'd better wipe the crumbs off your face."

Jessie smiled as Carole hastily wiped imaginary crumbs from her mouth. She listened to the light music penetrating the kitchen walls. Suddenly the doors burst open, and Amy appeared with an empty tray. Her face was flushed; her green eyes were blazing. She rested against the table and grabbed her chest in a dramatic show of heart palpitations.

"Are you okay?" Jessie asked, concerned.

Carole frowned. "Did Mr. Withers pinch your butt again?"

Amy shook her strawberry-blond head. "He's here," she said breathlessly.

Carole's brown eyes widened, then she grabbed her own chest. "He's here?" she whispered.

"Who's here?" Jessie asked.

The two women looked at her as if she had fallen from another planet.

"Mr. Perfect," Amy replied, forming the words in her mouth as if she were talking about a Greek god who had come to Earth on holiday.

Jessie resisted the urge to roll her eyes. "Oh, is that all?"

Unable to understand her disinterest in one of the most handsome and eligible bachelors on the entire East Coast, the two women ignored her.

Amy took another deep breath. "He is so gorgeous. His pictures don't do him any justice."

Carole reached for another tart, sighing loudly. "I know. He was good-looking in high school, but now..." She shook her head, trying to find the right words. "Now he's downright sinful."

Amy tucked a loose strand of hair behind her ear and leaned closer to Carole. "I asked him if he liked the food, and he looked right at me and said..." She paused, to heighten the climactic moment. "Yes." She fanned herself. "He's got the most beautiful brown eyes, and his voice...I thought I would faint dead away."

Jessie wished she could faint right then, so she wouldn't have to hear anymore about Mr. Perfect, aka Kenneth Preston. She tried to catch Wendy's attention so she would have an excuse to leave, but failed. Aside from the clattering of dishes and the shouted orders, the kitchen hummed with news about Kenneth's entrance.

She couldn't completely blame them. He was a home-town hero, a young man whose ingenuity and skill had brought new pride to Randall County, Maryland. He had been elected CEO of his boss's failing electronics company, and he had made it a multimillion-dollar success, creating jobs and bringing new investors to the area. But what more could you expect from a guy who was every parent's dream? The perfect son, the perfect student, the perfect date, the perfect everything. It made Jessie sick. Of course, it didn't help that they belonged to the same community.

In the Caribbean community, he was an idol. In a county proud of its ethnic diversity, the Caribbean community was quickly making its mark, and Kenneth Preston was its trump card. More times than Jessie could count, her mother would despair, wondering why Jessie couldn't be more like Kenneth. In a culture where your bragging rights are your social currency, Mrs. Clifton would have been bankrupt, had it not been for her two older daughters.

Like Carole, Jessie had grown up in Randall County and had firsthand experience with Mr. Perfect: falling for his charms and easy smile, and thinking him the perfect dream when he was actually the perfect nightmare. He was not what others thought, but attempting to convince anyone of that fact was fruitless, so she stayed out of his way and listened with disinterest to the stories that always circled around him. She knew otherwise. He was an arrogant, uptight jerk who would appear in hell wearing a three-piece suit just to keep up his image. Nobody had ever seen him in short sleeves, and only on rare occasions did he ever look unkempt.

"I can't believe he's not married yet," Amy said.

"Too busy having fun, I guess," Carole replied.

Amy drummed her fingers on the table. "I think he might be suffering from a broken heart. Remember that doctor he was seeing?"

"I heard he got bored with her."

"That was four years ago, and there hasn't been a woman since."

"I wouldn't be too sure. Rumor has it that he's dating his employees."

Amy shook her head. "No way. He wouldn't do that."

"He seems commitment-shy."

"He is a womanizer who collects hearts because he doesn't have one of his own," Jessie said. "Doesn't quite make him perfect, does it?"

They ignored her.

"I wish there were some way to get him to see me," Amy said.

Jessie handed her a tray of hors d'oeuvres. "It might help if you were up there in his field of vision, instead of down here talking about him."

"You're right," Amy replied, missing Jessie's bitter tone. "Oh, but you should have seen his date—"

Susan unexpectedly joined the group, like a camp leader

ready to put her troop in line. Her brown face was marred with a frown of displeasure. "Unless you're talking about how many glasses need refilling, or tarts that need to be heated, I suggest you ladies get to work."

Amy lifted a tray and backed out through the doors. Carole was reassigned to filling glasses, and Jessie was ordered to take a tray of them upstairs.

She reluctantly headed for the main ballroom through the underground tunnel, instead of the elevator. She hoped to be able to avoid Kenneth as long as possible, and hoped to act professional if she did run into him. She walked through the gray hallways, her shoes pounding against the white tile, and mused about the residents of the house. They probably weren't even aware that such an underground structure existed. It smacked of *Upstairs, Downstairs*. Them and Us. Kenneth had been an Us, and now he was a Them.

Not that she cared. She walked up the stairs, the music and voices growing louder. She wondered what it would be like to have a party in the middle of the week, and to have no worries, except what outfit to wear the next day. She thought of her sisters: Michelle busy at work and Teresa giving piano lessons. They didn't have the luxury of such impromptu soirees. When she reached the door to the main floor, she steadied her tray and lifted her head before entering.

She turned the corner and walked right into Mr. Perfect and the plateful of food he was holding. His meal smashed right into her uniform, like a pie in the face of a clown. Jessie lost her precarious hold on the tray full of glasses, and they fell to the ground with a shattering crash, spilling their contents like a broken aquarium.

"Why don't you watch where you're going?" she said, looking down at her ruined uniform and the broken glass.

He didn't offer her an apology; instead, a sour grin touched his face. "Figures it would be you."

She rested a hand on her hip, annoyed that Amy had been right. He did look gorgeous. His chestnut skin looked ravishing against the gunmetal gray of his shirt and his black trousers. He stood there staring at her with amused brown eyes, surrounded by an air of casual command that only a man blessed with his status could cultivate. She ground her teeth. "What's that suppose to mean?"

"It means that whenever you're around, disaster strikes."

"If you had been watching where you were going, this wouldn't have happened."

"Lower your voice," he ordered. "You're drawing attention..."

She lowered her voice to a deadly whisper. "I think what caught their attention was the shattering glass."

"Don't blame me. I'm not the one turning corners like I'm on a secret mission."

"Is that supposed to be some sort of explanation for throwing your food at me?"

"Throwing?" He lifted a dark eyebrow. "You walked right into me!"

She knew he was right, but she was too angry to calm down. She would not allow him the last word. "Well, you shouldn't have held it so clumsily. Or perhaps you could have had your latest concubine—I mean date—deliver it to you."

As if to add credence to her claim, a young woman, dressed in an outfit that could afford Jessie the down payment on a new luxury car, came up to Kenneth and possessively grabbed his arm. "What happened to you?" she asked Jessie, her lovely brown eyes genuinely concerned. Her parents had taught her that "the help" were people too, and she wanted to be sympathetic. She glanced down at the glasses. "You know, you really should get this cleaned up before someone gets hurt."

The woman had such a graceful, feminine manner that she made Jessie feel practically masculine. "That's clever of you to notice," she managed quietly.

She smiled, missing Jessie's sarcasm, and leaned towards Kenneth, her face in a pout. "I want to go home."

"In a minute," he said absently, his amused expression gone. "Go get something to drink."

"But—"

He stopped her with a hard look. She lowered her beautiful lashes and walked away.

"Looks like your date wants her nappy changed," Jessie muttered.

He shoved his hands in his pockets and stared at the ground. "Just for a minute, stop being a smartass and look at your left hand."

She lifted her hand and saw a pencil-thin cut slashed through her palm; a stream of blood seeped through and dripped onto the floor. Pain suddenly registered, but it was quickly replaced with an odd sense of annoyance. "Damn."

Kenneth handed her a crisp, white handkerchief, forcing her to apply pressure. Before she could argue, he turned away. "Clean up this mess, please," he told a passing waiter.

The waiter stopped and stared at the mess as if he had

come upon a car wreck and was being asked to provide emergency care. "But that's not my job."

Kenneth nodded and grinned. "Do you want to have a job?" His voice was soft; his threat was not.

The man swallowed. "I'll see what I can do."

"Thank you." Kenneth pointed to a woman in a maid's uniform, who was standing awkwardly in the doorway. "Get me some bandages and antibiotic ointment, please," he said, the hint of an island accent sweetening his words. The woman nodded and disappeared. He took hold of Jessie's other arm. "Come with me."

Trapped in his iron grip, she reluctantly followed him, inwardly groaning as she heard the crunch of broken glass under her feet.

In the powder room, he cleaned the cut, then had her press her hand against his in a fist.

"Does that hurt?"

She snatched her hand away. "Yes, of course!"

"Good. No nerve damage," he explained when she stared at him, outraged. "You've hurt yourself enough times to know the procedure."

"That's not true."

"You were the most reckless tomboy around. What do they call grown tomboys? 'Tommen'?"

"I am not a tomboy."

"Just afraid of being a woman, then?"

A timid knock interrupted her reply.

"Come in," he said.

The maid entered, staring at Kenneth with eyes of worship. She held out the bandages, her hand trembling, as though offering a famous celebrity a handmade gift. "Here are the bandages you needed."

"Thanks." He flashed one of his hundred-watt smiles. The woman blushed and shut the door. He turned to Jessie, and the smile disappeared.

Jessie felt both sickened and mesmerized by how quickly he could turn on the charm. She had to admit it was a gift. His smile made every woman believe he thought she was special, that she was number one in his life. Jessie knew: she had once been on the receiving end of one of those deceptive smiles. "Doesn't it get tiresome?"

He applied the ointment. "What?"

Jessie looked towards the ceiling, praying for patience. "The women."

He sent her an intense look, then began to gently wrap her hand. "You wouldn't believe me if I told you."

Jessie shrugged, indifferent. "You can wrap it tighter, you know," she said, annoyed by his tenderness. She just wanted him to wrap her hand and leave.

"I know. However, I must try to resist stopping your blood flow." He flashed a malicious grin. "The urge is tempting."

She made a face and surveyed the small powder room. Her gaze fell on the hand-painted violet-blossom tiles shipped in from Spain and the cobalt-blue-on-white china basin. She wished the room were larger, since Kenneth seemed to take up most of the free space and air. She could feel the heat from his body reach out and embrace her; the musky scent of his cologne played havoc with her senses. She began to feel lightheaded, which she was certain was a direct result of lost blood and eating only toast for breakfast. The flowers on the walls suddenly seemed to sway from an unknown breeze, and Kenneth felt far away—just the way she liked it. Then he was gone.

"Drink it," Kenneth demanded, shoving a glass of juice in her face.

"But I'm not—"

The glass was on her lips before she could finish her protest. She had the choice to either drink or choke. She chose the former. When she was through, she glanced around and realized she was sitting on a green camelback settee in the hallway, resting against Kenneth. She abruptly straightened.

"Put your head between your knees," he said.

"I'm not going to faint."

"You just did."

"I felt a little weak, but I was fine."

He folded his arms and rested back. "Hmm, I suppose admitting that you fainted would be too feminine for you."

"I have nothing against femininity. I am a woman, after all."

He measured her in one unflattering glance. "Not yet."

"What do you mean?"

He rubbed his chin, suddenly regretful. "Never mind."

"Say it."

He frowned, doubtful. "Do you really want me to explain?"

"If you can."

"Just look at yourself. You're not..." He didn't know how to complete the statement. She wasn't plain. Her skin was a rich dark brown, and her mouth was soft when she laughed, which she never did when he was around. But her eyes were killers, and whenever they flashed in his direction, a rush of heat would shoot through him. Why, he was never quite sure. Fortunately, he always managed to cool it.

No, she wasn't plain, but she wasn't pretty either. In a quick gesture, he lightly fingered the hair floating around her head. Even though she had attempted to pull her hair back in a braid, a few rebellious strands had broken free. He shook his head. "My *belle laide*," he said in a half-whisper.

"What?"

"Are you still reading *Madeline* to practice French?"

"I graduated to *Le Petit Prince*. Now, are you going to explain yourself or not?"

"You don't revel in being a woman. Your hair is always a mess, you hide your body in androgynous clothing—"

"This is a uniform, you idiot."

It hung on her like a sack; the arms were too long, as were the trousers. "And only you can make it look bad. It's like you don't even know the power of a woman's...attributes."

"I don't like fitted tuxes."

"Aside from the way you dress, any man who might be interested in you has to deal with your sharp tongue and nasty temper. The thought makes most men shudder."

"I see." She blinked back stinging, hot tears. It was her own fault. She had asked for honesty and received it in full. "It's nice to know what you really think of me. It explains everything."

He softened his voice, seeing the floating tears. "Jasmine—"

Her voice hardened. "Don't call me Jasmine."

He cradled her injured hand in his—a warm, solid hand that managed to make hers look small, helpless, almost delicate. Oh God, he was touching her, and her traitorous body enjoyed it. "We need to talk," he said.

She didn't want to talk to him. She didn't want to forgive him, like countless other brokenhearted females had. She hated how she had been weakened into bringing up the past in the first place. She had given him permission to carelessly tear at her wounds.

She hated that he could tap her weaknesses, while he kept his well-hidden. He could taunt her or make her feel foolish, but he could never know or understand how it felt to be her—not when he'd been given everything and had taken even more. He was a cunning illusion, trying to make her forget who he truly was. But she never would. She would not be another silent conquest of his deception. Without warning, an overwhelming need to hurt him, as he had hurt her, rose inside her.

She slapped him across the face so hard that her hand stung from the impact. She felt a secret delight when she saw his face become a violent storm, his eyes flashing with uncontrolled rage.

"Go on. Hit me back," she challenged. "I'm woman enough to take it. I know how much you want to. How much you truly despise me, because I know you're a fraud. I can see that temper of yours burning in your eyes, ready for release. Go on and act on impulse and show the world who you really are."

He grabbed her shoulders, lifting her off the settee, and she watched as he tried to keep himself from shaking her. He finally pushed her away from him. Jessie fell backwards, sitting down hard.

For a moment, Kenneth didn't breathe. He wouldn't allow his emotions to settle and take root. He knew the dangerous path down which untamed emotions could lead a man. He had perfected an iron will, which presently sought to douse the flames of his temper. He turned away. "I forgive you," he whispered in a harsh, raw voice that shook from an anger he was unsuccessfully trying to control.

"Don't you dare forgive me," she said, ready to see him break free from his magnanimous armor.

He spun around and grinned wickedly. All signs of anger were now hidden behind devilish eyes. "I forgive you," he said again, knowing this battle was his to win. "Do you want to try the other cheek?"

"You may be able to tame the savage beast, but I'll release it one day."

"Yes, but will you be able to deal with the consequences?"

A high-pitched shriek stopped her reply. "My beautiful glasses! Where is she? Where is that girl?"

Jessie leaped to her feet, alarmed. "Damn, that's Montey," she said in a panicked whisper. She looked around, desperate for a means of escape. She dashed behind a large plant. Kenneth rose to the occasion and moved in front of her and folded his arms, just in time to see Montey approach.

The guy is huge! Jessie thought, staring up at Kenneth's broad frame. He had the body of a warrior: solid arms, legs, and shoulders that could haul weapons and women. Being a big girl herself—and believing him to be one of Earth's lowest life-forms—she rarely noticed his size. *No wonder the jerk is so arrogant.*

Montey stopped in front of him. He was a bulky man with curly brown hair and a fussy mustache that bristled when he was agitated. It did so now. "Hello, Mr. Preston. Have you seen Jessie? I heard that she caused quite a disturbance. I'm glad that she didn't ruin your suit."

"No, she had a little accident."

"That girl *is* an accident," Montey said. "I never should have hired her. I was only doing her sister a favor."

"I'm sure she'll apologize."

"No more apologies. She's fired."

Jessie rested her forehead against the wall and groaned.

"What was that?" Montey asked.

Kenneth kicked the pot. "Oh, nothing."

"If you see Jessie, give her my message."

"I'm sure you could work something out."

Montey gave Kenneth a long, assessing look. "If you think she's such a good worker, perhaps you could give her a job." He spun on his heel and left.

Jessie sat and covered her face. Her shoulders shook. Kenneth reached for her, then thought better of it. "It will be okay."

She looked up at him, with tears of laughter.

"Did you hear him shriek?" she asked between breaths. "He sounds just like my grandmother when she gets angry. I never knew a man's voice could reach such a pitch." She wiped her tears away and sobered. "Damn, Michelle is going to kill me."

He sat down next to her. "Look, I can get you a job."

"Oh, no you don't," she said, shaking her head. She did

not want to receive any of his charity. "You've done enough." She shifted awkwardly. "Thanks for hiding me, though."

He shrugged.

She lifted her hand. "And for the bandage. Though I could have taken care of it myself."

He shrugged again.

Jessie looked at him, which was a mistake at so close a range. Up close, she noticed that his eyes were framed by curling black lashes that any woman would envy, and his full mouth entertained a shy smile. She also noticed an imprint forming on the side of his movie-star face: her handprint.

She swore. God had a nasty sense of humor. How could he make a man so beautiful and a woman so plain? "I am sorry about hitting you."

The corner of his mouth kicked up in a quick grin. "No, you're not."

"My temper gets the best of me sometimes," she continued, refusing to agree with him.

He raised an eyebrow. "Only sometimes?"

"I said I was sorry, but that's all I'll apologize for." She rested her elbows on her knees. "I mean, I know that I asked for it, but knowing that someone thinks you're a man doesn't put a person in a good mood."

"I've always thought of you as a woman, Jas. I'm just waiting for you to."

It was a line of bull, and she was falling for it, diving into his delicious chocolate eyes and allowing his words to cascade over her like a waterfall. He was the most convincing sheep-clad wolf she had ever met.

"I still don't like you," she said.

His mouth spread to a full grin, the one he saved for special occasions. Her pulse quickened. She ignored it.

"Fair enough," he said. "I don't like you either."

For a moment they shared a gaze and a camaraderie that began to change into something more intimate as they stared at each other. He unexpectedly brushed a finger against her cheek, then put it in his mouth. "You had whipped cream on your face," he whispered. "I'm hungry."

She rubbed where his finger had been. "Then get something to eat. I don't want you eating off of me."

"Don't worry. I realize poison is deadly."

She sent him a rude glance, which she reluctantly softened with a smile. "Touché." She turned away and stood, breaking the sudden awareness that had come between them. "Looks like your date wants you."

Kenneth also stood, frowning. He watched his date approach. "You might have been right about the nappy thing. She does act like a baby." He turned to see Jessie's reaction, but she was gone.

ABOUT THE AUTHOR

Dara Girard, an award-winning, national bestselling author of more than forty novels, from romance to suspense, loves telling stories.

Born in the US to immigrant parents, Dara enjoys pulling from her Jamaican, British, Nigerian heritage and exposure to various cultures to bring what reviewers and fans call "vivid emotional stories" to life. She is best known for her popular Henson Series, the mysterious Clifton Sisters, and the fun Black Stockings Society.

You can write her at:

contactdara@daragirard.com

Visit her website to sign up for her newsletter and get sneak peeks, monthly updates on new releases, and special offers.

For more information visit
www.daragirard.com